HONEYMOON SWEET

AN OUT & ABOUT NOVEL

ALLISON TEMPLE

HONEYMOON SWEET

Doug is a cheese pizza kind of guy. A honeymoon cruise around the Caribbean is the most adventurous thing he's ever done. Going on that honeymoon alone is unthinkable, but here he is, with a luxury suite and a broken heart.

Tripp is a hopeless romantic. He's in a sinking relationship that's been taking on water for months. He'd throw in the towel if he had one, but he's naked and locked out of his room.

No one should be on a cruise alone, and Tripp has a simple solution: he and Doug will pretend to be husbands and enjoy everything a week of sea and sun has to offer. But as the days and nights heat up, can a cheese pizza kind of guy be brave enough to give love a second chance?

Honeymoon Sweet is a 63k contemporary MM romance. It's sweet enough to require a trip to the dentist, and hot enough you'll need a swim to cool off when it's over. HEA guaranteed.

Copyright © 2020 by Allison Temple
Honeymoon Sweet
All rights reserved. ISBN 978-1-7753144-9-3

No part of this book may be reproduced in any form or by any electronic or mechanical means, including information storage and retrieval systems, without written permission from the author, except for the use of brief quotations in a book review.

This is a work of fiction. Names, characters, places, and incidents are a product of the author's imagination or are used fictitiously. Any resemblance to actual events, places, or persons, living or dead, is entirely coincidental.

Cover Design: Samantha Santana, AMAI Designs
Developmental Editing: Posy Roberts, Boho Press
Copy Editing: Manuela Velasco, Tessera Editorial
Proofreading: Kiki Clark, LesCourt Author Services

 Created with Vellum

For the romantics. May you find someone who loves you for you, cheese pizza and all.

For news on future releases, join the A-List (allisontemplebooks.com/newsletter), my monthly newsletter.

1

DOUG

The naked man in the hall is icing on the surreal cake that has been the past forty-eight hours of my life. Calvin would probably say it's because my libido has basically shrivelled to nothing, but it's mostly because I'm completely lost and so busy trying to remember my suite number that the glowing gleam of the stranger's ass, practically pink against long tanned legs and a gently muscled spine, is literally a foot in front of me before I notice it.

"Oh my God!" I clap a hand over my eyes and gasp like a homecoming dance chaperone. Except I leave a space open between my fingers, for whatever reason, so I get an eyeful when he turns towards me with a shocked expression that melts to horror.

Along with his tight body, he's rocking a decent-sized package.

Not that I look.

Except I do, mostly to prove to Calvin that I am not a monk after all.

"Oh fuck!" His voice is deeper than I expected, and it hits my chest in a nice way. Better than the twisting anxiety that's basically been gnawing there like a rabid squirrel since yesterday. When I spread my fingers open again, he's got one hand over his crotch, and he's sort of half twisted away from me, like he can't decide if it's worse to show me his ass or his palm barely covering his dick.

"Uh. Sorry. Sorry." I try to step around him. Cruise ship halls are narrow, and we get closer than is probably strictly appropriate in this suddenly clothing-optional environment. He smells like coconut and sunscreen.

"Yeah," he says. It's like we're on magnets. As I pass, he keeps rotating, so I never lose the quarter view of his ass and the growing pink that's spreading up his neck. It must be contagious, because my ears are pulsing like a furnace.

I'm ten steps up the hall when I hear his heavy sigh. The sound sends a shiver up my neck. I've made it a lot myself lately.

He's facing away from me, hands on his hips, ass clenched tight. Whoever comes around that corner next is going to get quite the show. But then his shoulders slump, and I know that disappointed defeat intimately.

"Can I—" What am I supposed to say? "Can I help you? With something?"

His head turns slightly, chin dipping over his shoulder. His hair is dark blond and a little spiked at the tips, just like his nose and jaw are sharp like an angry bird's. Not an Angry Bird. An actual unhappy bird. Like how a crow stares at you like you've interrupted its lunch.

"Sorry," I say when the silence goes on too long. "Never mind."

"I'm locked out of my room," that too-deep voice says. His eyes flick to mine, and he gives this smile that says he knows I'm staring at his ass, and he knows it's a nice ass. I try to speak so fast I bite my tongue and hiss, putting a hand to my mouth while my eyes fill with tears.

It's nice to cry about physical pain for a change.

He's still watching me, so I swallow and say, "Have you checked your pockets?"

The whir of the air conditioning is not nearly loud enough to hide my humiliation. Nothing is these days.

He snorts out a soft laugh. "Funny guy. I don't suppose you can get me a towel or something?"

I look around me, momentarily confused. Unlike him, I *do* have pockets, but surely he can see all I have to offer is a polo shirt and cargos.

He bumps his forehead against what I assume is the door to his room. "Never mind."

His room . . .

"Oh! Yeah. Come down to my suite. I can get you something to, um—" My eyes will not stay off his body. "Cover up with."

He scrubs his fingers through the back of his hair where it's cut short along his nape. What's the appropriate thing to do? Should he walk back to my room with me—assuming I remember where it is—and risk meeting other people as we go, or should he stay here?

"It's this way," I say, because it feels wrong to leave him—er —hanging here himself.

He bobs up and down on his toes a couple times, but then voices echo from the direction I've come, and that seems to decide for him, because he spins towards me.

"Lead the way, Magellan."

I head down the hall like I know where I'm going. His bare feet are very close behind me, probably so I can shield him from any unfortunate on-comers. People behind us will still get a view, but he's clearly chosen the lesser of two evils on this.

Finally—and without meeting anyone else, thank goodness —I spot the door with the St. Patrick's Day leprechaun taped to it. Our—my suite is the one opposite, but I'd heard this was a

thing people do on cruises, to help them find their way. I'd
suggested doing something similar to Calvin, but he'd reminded
me we were adults who should be able to remember a simple
number sequence.

Except it turns out that when your fiancé leaves you at the
altar, your mental state is so scattered that even a four-digit
number is hard to keep track of. Thank fuck for Kelly green
paper leprechauns with sparkly bowties.

My room is opposite the pot of gold, and I let myself have a
single sigh of relief when I wave the key card over the sensor and
the lock whirs.

I realize my mistake the second I push open the door.

"Wow," he says. "It's huge."

Big enough for two, I almost say. Instead I keep my eyes
down as I rush to the bathroom and fumble for a towel, even
though cruise ship towels are not made for public consumption.
If he even manages to get it wrapped around his waist, it'll be
like a skirt with a slit that would make a Hollywood starlet
blush. And Mr. In-the-Buff needs more than that to go down-
stairs and ask for a new room key, if he wants the thirty-six
hundred passengers on the Tropical Vista to remain unscan-
dalized.

"I think I saw a couple robes in the closet." I definitely saw
them, but the sight of a *couple* anything is enough to make my
throat hurt, so I'd closed it without giving it a second thought.

He's not standing by the door, which at least makes it easy to
wrestle one of the robes off its hanger, but the fact remains, a
strange naked man is now somewhere in my room, which is far
more stressful and far less exciting than it should be.

He's on the balcony.

"Way to make yourself at home," I grumble, and the quiet
indignation is a kind of relief after the endless barrage of misery
since the chapel doors opened and no one was there.

His back is to me, with one foot crossed behind the other, and he's got his hands spread out on the rail. A shaft of sunlight is playing over his hair and shoulders, showing off his tan. He looks way more comfortable than I felt when I went to inspect the view earlier. We are a long way up, and I am afraid of heights.

"Here," I say as I push the sliding door open. He smiles as he reaches for it. His modesty seems to be gone, like he doesn't care that I can see him. Kind of the way Calvin treated me like I was invisible for those last months of wedding planning, when he said it would all be easier if I let him make the decisions.

Better to be invisible, though, than to have 120 sets of eyes trained on you as everyone simultaneously reaches the same horrifying conclusion. The jazz guitarist kept playing the processional Calvin painstakingly chose. It should have been the song etched into my head the first time I saw my husband on our wedding day, but we all knew the truth.

Calvin wasn't coming.

"Thanks." The naked man is no longer naked. He's got the robe tied snuggly around his waist, although it's still open enough that I can see the sprinkling of gold-brown hair on his chest.

"You're welcome." My smile feels weird on my face, like I haven't smiled in weeks.

"I'm Tripp," he says, holding out his hand. When I shake it, his grip is firm, and I want to lean into it while the breeze on the balcony ripples through my clothes and makes me feel more exposed than he was until very recently.

"Tripp." Wasn't there a character in *The Philadelphia Story* named Tripp? Surely Carey Grant played a Tripp at some point. "I'm Doug. Er . . . Douglas . . . Dougie. Just—" I clear my throat. "Doug. It's nice to meet you."

"Thanks for the robe, Dougie Douglas. I'll bring one back

for you." He glances at my hand. "Tell your wife this was sacri-ficed for a good cause."

I go cold as words fall out of my mouth like vomit. "Oh, no. I'm not—I don't have a wife—I'm gay. My husband is—I mean my fiancé—" Every syllable is like another nail in my coffin.

He gives me a flirty up-and-down look. I want to put my hands over my body to try to cover myself, like he did, even though I'm fully dressed.

"Good for you, Dougie. Tell your man I'll send a replacement robe as soon as I get back into my room."

I don't say anything else, because the truth is, I only need one robe. Everything in this room is arranged in pairs. Two robes, two sets of towels, two champagne glasses placed next to the bucket now filled with water, because I let the ice melt hours ago. No point in keeping the champagne chilled; I have nothing to celebrate.

Tripp's watching me, and there's a now-familiar sting in the corners of my eyes, so I say, "No problem. He won't be needing it."

He smiles, and his eyebrows arch as he nods. "Yeah, honey-moon, eh?" He bites his lower lip. "I get it. Who needs clothes, right?"

My self-esteem dies a little more, which is saying something, to know there's still any left to lose after everything. "Right."

The wind teases the tie of his robe, and I have to look away, out over the glistening water. The sun's going down. I keep my eyes on the horizon, ignoring the thought of how high up we are.

Maybe I'll drink the whole bottle of champagne myself. It's not like I'm rushing off to a cozy candlelit dinner.

Tripp has a hand on the sliding door. "I'll let myself out."

"Oh. Yeah. Of course." My manners say I should walk him to the door, but why? This isn't my house. He's not some friend I've invited over. I'll probably never see him again. My plan for the next eight days is to get thoroughly lost in the crowd so I don't have to dwell on the fact that I'm alone.

The click of the latch says he's gone, and I didn't even say goodbye.

2

TRIPP

So, you're probably wondering how a guy locks himself out of his room while he's naked on a cruise ship.

It goes something like this:

Step 1: Fly the red-eye from Vancouver to Miami, only to get diverted at the last minute to Fort Lauderdale when a freak thunderstorm closes the Miami airport.

Step 2: Nearly miss your cruise departure when your plane sits on the tarmac at FLL for four hours before finally getting clearance to return to MIA.

Step 3: Lose your luggage somewhere between North Van and SoFlo. Argue with the baggage agent who says it could be four to six days before your bags catch up with you. Talk her down to two but know that you've used up your annual allotment of karma points in the process.

Step 4: Race onto the ship literally moments before they roll up the gangway, running on maybe an hour of sleep in the last two days, because you never sleep well on planes and jetlag is a bitch.

Step 5: Have an explosive fight with your boyfriend— possibly about whose fault all of the above is, but really, when has Liam ever needed a reason to start an argument when he's

8

flustered?—while wearing only a towel, after you shower in a tiny cruise cabin bathroom in a futile effort to wash all the stress and sweat off.

Step 6: Chase after said boyfriend when he storms out with his usual flair for the dramatic, only to lose your towel just at the threshold of the cabin.

Step 7: Listen in horror as the door clicks shut behind you, with your towel on one side and you on the other.

Bonus points if the person who discovers you standing stark naked is an adorable bear cub on his honeymoon.

After the group ahead of me at guest services, featuring two sobbing children, an irate mom in Gucci sunglasses, and a dad who won't put his phone down while his wife berates the poor woman behind the desk because their ocean view room doesn't have the bunk beds she promised her children, my sheepish request for a new ship pass probably seems like a relief. The woman doesn't even bat an eye when I show up in my borrowed bathrobe and no shoes to say I've locked myself out of my room. She checks my picture against the one they took when we got on board, then promptly hands me a replacement card, which I tuck into the pocket of the robe.

Of course, Liam is back in our room when I return. He likes to make an exit, but without our usual cadre of friends to circle the wagons and console him, no doubt he did one lap of the pool deck, realized no one cared about his blotchy face, and came back so he could continue sulking once I returned.

He's lying on the bed, his back to me. He's also right in the middle of the mattress, which is basically a dare. Our fight started when he announced I would have to sleep on the right side of the bed—which I never do at home—because I'm shorter than he is and the bottom right corner has been cut away slightly to make it easier to get around it and out to the balcony. And while this may not sound like a big deal, it is to me, because I like to sleep on my right shoulder—I screwed up my left one playing lacrosse in high school, back when I thought anyone would buy my straight jock persona—but that only works if it means I'm facing away from Liam so he can't breathe on my face all night.

The fight was not my finest moment, I'll admit, but we were both exhausted. So when I told Liam I would be sleeping on the left side of the bed because it is my side, he flipped out and called me inconsiderate, and the next thing I knew he was gone and I was naked, and now we're all caught up.

He shifts, knees bending under the sheets, which is his way of letting me know he's awake and ready to hear my apology.

I grind my teeth. We're excellent at freezing each other out. Last summer, after a fight about the best way to cook flank steak, Liam didn't talk to me for almost a week. After the third day, it actually became kind of relaxing.

But we're on this trip to try to get away from the drama of day-to-day life, and launching into the silent treatment while we aren't even a hundred miles from Florida is not a great way to start.

"I'm glad you came back," I say softly as I slide into bed, spooning behind him. He's stiff in my arms.

"Where was I going to go?"

At least he can't see the way I roll my eyes before I say, "Should we go explore? Grab a drink? The daily schedule says there's an LGBT-plus mixer at five?"

He rolls a little farther away from me, towards the side of the bed he said he didn't want. "I'd rather stay here."

"I can get on board with that." I cuddle closer, pressing myself along his back. I hate this kind of emotional bargaining, but if it will get him to look at me, I'll do it.

He pushes my hand away when I stroke his hip. "Think I just want to sleep."

I sigh. We've had our problems lately, but Liam's never not been interested in sex before.

"Baby?" I croon, but when he doesn't move, I don't pursue it. If he doesn't want me, that's fine. With a whole ship out there, if he wants to sulk, I'll go entertain myself.

I kiss the back of his neck with all the heat I would put into kissing my grandma. "I'll come find you for dinner."

"I might be in the business center."

His words make me freeze, mid-roll off the bed. The robe falls open over my legs, leaving my dick hanging out for the second time in the last hour, and once again I feel like an idiot.

"But you promised," I say, trying not to whine.

"There was an email from Mae before, while we were waiting in Fort Lauderdale."

Of course there was. Mae is Liam's business partner, and she, like him, must have had her smartphone surgically attached to her hand, because they are never out of contact. And anything one sends the other automatically becomes priority number one.

I have been trying to compete with Mae's emails since Liam and I met. This cruise is my last hope. If I can't get him to look at me while we're hundreds of miles from everything and internet access costs a buck a minute, then what chance do I have?

He finally rolls towards me. I pull the robe closed over my lap, but his hand finds my calf. "It'll just be this one thing. The Singapore distributor is threatening to pull out. I just need to smooth it over, and then I'm all yours." He gives me his best smile, the one that used to make my knees weak and my dick hard, but in the last few months, it just makes me feel like a cat chasing a laser pointer.

I give him *my* best smile in return, because we are going to *try* on this trip. "Yeah. Okay. I'll go find you there later."

Man, a cruise ship is *huge*. I keep forgetting I'm not in a hotel. I barely feel the boat moving as I walk from one end to the other, and the giant atrium and endless shops feel less like a boat and more like one of those Vegas casinos Liam took me to last year.

I grab a mojito at the bar—hello, unlimited alcohol package—and make my way to the LGBT-plus mixer, but it's not really my scene. It's a pretty diverse group, both age- and gender-wise, but the men are mostly old bears and daddies here to ogle the much younger man candy and buff dudes looking to arrange their on-board hookups. The old guys are nice, although they'd like me better if I spoke less and flexed more. The younger guys eye me with a hunger I've seen too many times at clubs and bars, but I'm here to patch things up with my boyfriend, and he's never liked to share.

I see Doug, for second, at the far end of the room. He's just kind of . . . standing there, staring out a big window as the ocean rolls by. I watch him, expecting the newly minted Mr. Doug to appear with drinks for both of them and a kiss for Doug, but no one does. Doug might as well not be there at all. But just as I'm about to walk over and thank him again for rescuing me and my dignity, two women with blue hair and a ton of tattoos bump into me, getting their pink slushy drinks on my shirt. We do the usual dance of "I'm so sorry" and "no, it's really okay," even though this is literally my only shirt until we get to Mexico, and by the time I look towards the window again, Doug is gone.

I go up to the business centre at ten after eight. Liam is hunched over a keyboard, angrily smashing at keys, while his forehead tries to recreate the topography of the Grand Canyon as he frowns.

"Ready for dinner?" I say, trying to keep my voice casual. He grunts and clicks through more screens. My stomach growls audibly, and Liam glares at me like I've let a child run amok in a funeral.

"Give me a half hour." His attention goes back to the screen.

No. No. This is the dance we do at home. Another half hour. Which becomes an hour, and then two hours, and then dinner is cold and I'm watching Netflix by myself until I fall asleep on the couch.

Nights like that are why I begged Liam to come on this vacation, and already I'm starting to wonder why. My best friend, Pierce, always says you can't throw money at personal problems, and he has enough of it—money, not problems—that he would know. But this cruise cost a lot of money, and I need it to be worth the investment.

"Babe." I put a hand on his shoulder. We made promises. Agreed on terms. He is not keeping up his end.

He blinks up at me, and I can see the conflict. If we were home, I would lose this fight without another word being spoken, but just as my spine starts to stiffen, he smiles and says, "Yeah. Yeah, let's eat."

Dinner is . . .

I don't want to call it a disaster, because we're both tired, so it's understandable if we don't have one of those deep conversations that will change the course of our mutual future. But once we're through the chitchat about what we want to eat and whether we should order a whole bottle of wine, Liam and I both . . . stare.

"I really didn't think we were going to make it," I say.

He gives a half smile. "Yeah. If we'd gotten stuck in Fort Lauderdale, I would have just turned around and gone home."

I'm about to take a drink, and my hand jerks as he finishes speaking, making the water drip down my chin. "What?"

He raises an eyebrow. "Come on, Tripp. We planned to go on a cruise, not chase a cruise around the Caribbean."

I'm aghast. "You would have given up? Just like that?" We've been planning this trip for months. Or rather, I've been planning, and Liam's been nodding from behind his laptop when I tell him about the ship's features and our destinations. I told myself he'd be into it once we got here.

"Well, we'd have lost, what? Two days?" he says.

"Yeah! What's two days?" We'd have caught a flight to

Mexico. How bad could that be? Margaritas and tacos while we wait for the ship to pick us up on its first stop.

He shakes his head. Runs a hand over the tablecloth. His thumb is making circles in the air, and I realize it's the motion of him swiping through his phone.

"Oh my God," I say, disbelieving.

"What?" His hand freezes.

"You don't even have your phone on you. Are you that addicted? You can't even sit and have dinner with me?"

He rolls his eyes. "Don't be dramatic."

"Dramatic?" My voice rises despite all my good intentions.

"Right this way, sir," a dining room host says, and I look up just in time to see him pull out a chair at the table next to ours, and what do you know? Here's my saviour yet again. Dougie Douglas sits down, giving the host and Liam an uncomfortable smile before his gaze lands on me, and his eyes go wide.

"Oh. Hi," he says. He has a nice face. Kind, my mom would say. His beard is well trimmed, and his brown hair is maybe a little thin on the top, but he's got it cut short enough that you can't really tell. He seems nervous, but since his first introduction to me was my bare ass and more, I get why he might not be quite sure what to do right now.

Liam asks, "You two know each other?"

"Yeah!" I say before Doug can fill in too many details. "Doug's staying down the hall from us."

Liam eyes me, like he knows I've glossed over something, but Doug has picked up his menu and is reading it very closely, clearly indicating he wants to be left alone.

His presence keeps Liam and me on better behavior, though. We talk about the food—which is amazing—and what we think we might do tomorrow. Liam orders a bottle of wine, and even though I can't pronounce the words on the label, I do my best to drink my fair share, since it's already paid for. Liam doesn't mention work and doesn't say no when I suggest I'll book a couple's massage.

Only when our main courses have arrived and I'm focusing on my food do I realize Doug is still sitting by himself. I'd have thought someone would join him, but also, I was so focused on having a nice time with Liam that I sort of blocked out the tables around us. But now that we're eating and the conversation has dropped off again, I notice Doug is quietly picking at his Caesar salad at a table for one.

"You wear him out?" I say.

Doug's fork clatters to his plate. "Sorry?"

Liam snorts. "Don't be crude."

I smile. "Your husband. Was he too tired to come down to dinner?"

Doug gapes at me. "I—"

"Newlyweds," I say to Liam. "A cruise would be a great honeymoon, wouldn't it?"

He shrugs. "I guess."

"Maybe we can go on another cruise after we get married."

The suggestion is out of my mouth before I've even thought about it, and the implication of what I've just said dawns on me with the same suddenness as undisguised shock crashes on Liam's face.

"Excuse me," Doug says, pushing up from his table so fast his glassware rattles, but I'm not looking at him, because all I can see is the naked horror on my boyfriend's face at the very idea that I might want to marry him someday.

"Tripp . . . I . . . " He takes a long drink of his wine.

My heart is pounding in my chest as I force a smile. "Oops," I say. "Too many daiquiris before dinner. You know I didn't mean that." I didn't. I was just trying to say something clever to ease the tension rolling off Doug in waves, and now look what I've done. Liam's posture and his face are a glittering firework of *hell no,* and it hurts more than I expected. If he's that opposed to the idea, what is he even doing with me? What am I doing with him?

After that, I think we can safely say the rest of dinner is a disaster. Liam skips dessert and coffee and says he has to go check his email again, and I'm so busy backtracking every moment in our relationship, wondering where it all went wrong or if it was ever right to start with—I can't even protest.

3

DOUG

*C*oming here was a mistake. After Calvin broke up with me by text exactly fourteen minutes after he was supposed to walk down the aisle, I was so out of it that when my mom and my sisters said the best thing for me to do was get on the plane to Florida and take the week to wipe the slate clean, the suggestion sounded reasonable.

Except even though I'm out on the open ocean where the horizons stretch forever, I've never been deeper inside my head. Every single thing on this ship is here to remind me that I'm not supposed to be alone. Calvin said he wanted to plan the wedding, but I could do whatever I wanted for our honeymoon.

So I did. I planned it all. I pored over endless reviews for every cruise line and then for every ship. I looked at weather data. I left posts on message boards. The next seven days have been planned as meticulously as the minute-by-minute game plan of our wedding that Calvin made me memorize.

But no part of my plan involved me being here by myself.

I try to follow my family's advice and leave my cabin in the afternoon. There's a queer meet and greet, but the second I walk in, I know it's a mistake, because the first thing someone says to me is "you're here alone?" No one goes on a cruise alone.

And hell, when it comes to socializing, I've hardly been anywhere without Calvin in more than two years. We were inseparable, and now I feel like I'm missing the most interesting part of me.

I think about ordering room service and just never leaving my suite again but decide to try one more time at dinner. Unfortunately, I got seated right next to Tripp and his model-gorgeous boyfriend. When Tripp makes a joke about how I must have worn Calvin out with my legendary sexual prowess, all I can think is that, instead, I managed to drive him away without even knowing why.

I try to hold it together, enjoy my dinner, but I'm done. Tripp and his boyfriend are still talking, but their words are all static in my ears. I go back to my room, pull the blankets over my head, and shut out the world.

The next day starts unbearably early. I've made up my mind to talk to someone about getting off the cruise in Mexico and flying home, but I thought I'd avoid most of today by sleeping. So it's irritating when I'm woken up at eight o'clock by a projected *bong bong* through the public address system, after which an overly perky cruise director tells me all about the amazing things he has planned for the day to keep us entertained.

And once he's done, the silence floods back in, and all I can do is stare at the ceiling and wonder how I could have possibly missed that the man who had promised to spend the rest of his life with me couldn't even make it one day.

On Christmas morning, after all the presents have been opened, and my nieces and nephews are finally quiet, engaged in games and new tablets, Calvin produces one last box. It's wrapped in red paper and fits in the palm of my hand, and I know what it is immediately. My mom has tears in her eyes when I open it, and I cry a bit too when I see Dad's gold band inside.

"Doug Freeman, will you marry me?" Calvin smiles at me from

where he's kneeling in front of the couch, and finally everything is going to be okay in my life again.

A knock on the suite door nearly has me jumping out of my skin, but when I open the door, it's a cruise staff member wearing a white jacket and a friendly smile. "Good morning, Mr. Freeman."

I feel hungover, even though the sum total of what I had to drink last night was about two sips from a glass of wine before Tripp accidentally sent me running from dinner. Maybe I'm dehydrated.

"Can I bring your breakfast in?"

I realize I'm standing in the narrow door and blocking the way of the man carrying a very wide tray of covered dishes.

"Oh, yes, sorry." I step aside and let him bring it in. Vaguely, I remember filling in the card the night before to order in-room breakfast. I was so busy drowning in sadness that I'm not totally sure what's under the covers, but I have a hunch it's ninety percent carbs.

"Sweetheart, don't you want to look amazing for our pictures?"

The first time Calvin asked me that was at lunch in our condo on a Sunday afternoon. I'd made a grilled cheese, and Calvin looked at it like it contained arsenic. The question was such a contrast to the months after my dad died and he would beg me to eat anything that I didn't know what to say.

Now, I groan when I lift the silver domes off each plate. Pancakes, French toast, bacon, sausage, croissants. There's a silver pot that must be coffee next to two big glasses of orange juice. I grab the first one and suck half of it down without a second thought.

"Will your husband be back soon?"

I snort orange juice right out my nose. The server is super nice about it, offering napkins and apologizing profusely.

"My husband?" I say.

"The other Mr. Freeman?" He looks apologetic, no doubt

because dry-land drowning guests is frowned upon in the employee manual. "If he won't be back right away, I can take his breakfast back down. Or you can keep it covered."

Shame swamps me, and I slump on the suite's couch. "It's fine," I say, still mopping at my face. Everything smells like orange juice. "He'll be right back."

I eat all the French toast, half the pancakes, and crush the croissants into dust, only eating the fluffy white bits in the middle. I'm clearly off orange juice for the foreseeable future, but the coffee isn't bad.

I'm finally starting to feel human when raised voices from out in the hall echo through my door.

"Oh, don't be like that. It'll only take me an hour."

"An hour? An hour? You said an hour last night, and what time did you come to bed?"

"It was the middle of the day in Singapore. Those are prime working hours."

"You're not supposed to be working, Liam. You're supposed to be here, with me." His voice breaks, and my heart squeezes at the sound.

"Well, fuck. If I'd known you were going to expect me at your beck and call—"

"It's a vacation! We're supposed to spend time together."

I'm standing right behind the suite door. Part of me feels like I should stick my head out, not because I want to see the show, but because the fight is making my heart do funny things, and if they don't go away, I feel like I'm going to start crying again and never stop.

"Tripp, don't be needy."

"Babe, don't be like that. You're a big boy."

"I'm not being needy, I'm sticking to the plan. Do you want to be here with me or not?"

"Doug, are you okay? I don't have to go to work if you need me to stay home."

I don't know which Calvin to listen to and the clash of memories makes my head spin. I can't do anything about them, and I need something to give. I open the door with a click. I'm only in boxers and a torn Out & About T-shirt, but since I'm one hundred percent more clothed than Tripp was yesterday, I figure I'm good.

They're both standing in the narrow hall. Tripp's boyfriend has his back to me, but he turns as I poke my head out. He . . . does not look like someone on vacation. I'd assumed he'd dressed up for dinner last night or that maybe he's the kind of guy who likes to go business casual when he flies, but he's still in pressed pants and a collared shirt this morning, while Tripp is in a graphic tee and shorts.

The boyfriend gives me a polite smile with no hint of embarrassment, like he's about to ask me for a grande no-foam latte. Instead he says, "Excuse me," and walks away. I watch him go for a second, before my attention swings back to Tripp. He's standing in the hall, arms crossed over his chest. His face is mottled with colour, and his shoulders bob up and down as he breathes heavily. He brings his hand to the back of his neck.

"Sorry about that," he says.

I almost tell him he should be glad he's got someone who still wants him enough to argue instead of making unilateral decisions and vanishing, but just because I'm suddenly privy to details of his personal life doesn't necessarily mean he wants the same from me.

Instead, I ask, "Do you want some coffee?"

He looks me up and down before a lazy grin spreads over his face. "At least I'm wearing clothes this time." Then he plucks at his T-shirt. "Yesterday's clothes."

"Yesterday's?" I say as I lead him back into the suite.

"The airline lost our bags. Or, sorry, they're not lost, just 'delayed.'" He says the last part while making air quotes. "They weren't delayed. It's not like they got stuck in traffic. They were supposed to get on the flight to Miami, and instead they wound up going to Toronto.”

My head pops up from where I’m arranging coffee cups on the table. “I’m from Toronto.”

He cocks his head to one side. “Really? We’re—I’m from Vancouver.”

I can’t help my smile as I ask, “Do you know Bob?”

Tripp grins at the joke every Canadian knows. “Bob from Vancouver?”

“Yeah.”

“Yeah! He’s my neighbor.”

Canada. The biggest small country in the world.

He gives me a nod as I hand him a mug, which he then empties six sugar packets into before taking a sip and smiling. I watch him, feeling a little nauseous, and his eyes get nervous when he catches me staring. “What?”

“There’s less sugar in a can of Coke.”

He shrugs. “Liam likes his coffee to basically be the consistency and flavour of roofing tar. I’m used to having to sweeten it a lot.”

“That’s your boyfriend?” I ask. He nods, but he doesn’t look happy about it. “He seems very . . . important.”

“He’s a designer.”

I was expecting lawyer or banker, but maybe that’s just all my years with Calvin showing through. “He’s successful?”

Tripp snorts. “More and more all the time. I met him at a show last year. He designs high-end menswear—suits and things. He’s just started selling in Asia.”

“And he doesn’t like vacations?” I bite my lip, hoping that question isn’t too personal.

“No, he does!” Tripp shakes his head vigorously, but then catches the movement and slumps again. “He’s just been really busy lately.”

He won’t quite meet my eyes, and I know that feeling. How

many times did I tell people that Calvin wished he could be there, but he's really busy? Or thought that maybe the whole wedding thing was overblown, and we should just go to city hall on a Tuesday and sign the papers, and then we'd be okay?

"No, babe. We need this. A milestone to mark the start our life together."

Except the before and after of my life feels like it's always going to be when Dad died. I didn't need a wedding, just a husband to hold me when the grief got to be too much, and Calvin was already that.

"Not tonight, babe. I'm tired."

Except sometimes when he wasn't, but we all have our off nights, right?

"Have you been on a cruise before?" I ask.

Tripp's looking across the bed and through the balcony window, but he shrugs and turns back to me. "First time. You?"

"Yup." I'd picked it because it seemed like a low-effort way to unwind after the wedding. Calvin said all-inclusive resorts were tacky, and I knew he'd have rather hiked the Camino de Santiago or something, but I was not going to be up for that after the seemingly endless rotation of suit fittings and cake tastings.

"Got plans for when we get to Cozumel?"

"I booked the tequila tour. You?"

He pours himself fresh coffee and repeats the sugaring. "Liam said we'd figure it out when we got there. He said there were always independent tour operators looking to pick people up at the ports."

That kind of unformed schedule makes me twitchy. I almost say they can have my tickets. I'm flying home tomorrow. Back to the condo Calvin and I shared for the past three years so I can—

Oh no. What happens now? The condo is in both our names. Someone needs to move. I don't have the cash to buy Calvin out, but if the condo doesn't sell fast, I won't have enough to bridge a mortgage on a second place either. So I guess that means Calvin has to buy me out. Where will I go? I've lived in that corner of Leslieville for more than ten years. But all of the little places, the coffee shops and pubs, the ones I thought of as mine before Calvin moved in, have become ours. They know our coffee orders and that Calvin prefers Syrah in the winter and rosé in the summer. How will I ever be able to walk back in there again?

I'm going to be sick. My body is going into cold and hot flashes, and my hands are shaking. I can't go home. Can't face the people there. My family. Friends and co-workers. What will I tell the baristas?

"So, what's your deal?"

It's like I'm looking through someone else's eyes as I focus on Tripp again.

"Excuse me?"

He gives me a sheepish smile. "Sorry if this is personal, but . . . You said you were on your honeymoon, didn't you? Or that you had a husband at least. But, like." He jerks a thumb over his shoulder towards the bed. "Only one side of the covers are messed up, and there's only one suitcase in the corner. And the other robe is still hung up on the closet door there. So I was just wondering . . . "

He doesn't finish, because each word is like a slowly twisting knife to my insides that catalogues every single one of my insecurities and shame.

I do the only thing I can do.

I burst into tears.

4

TRIPP

So, look. I know one of the supposed benefits of embracing your gay identity is escaping the shackles of toxic masculinity and all the emotional constipation that goes with that, but:

A) That's a shitty stereotype because all stereotypes are shitty.

B) I still suck at feelings. And now I've made Dougie Doug cry.

C) Doug has clearly embraced his emotional landscape far better than I have.

He's really crying. Like full-on, snot-faced, hiccupping-while-your-face-slowly-goes-purple crying. It's ugly and messy and, even if I didn't intend to be, I'm somehow responsible for this, and so it's also my responsibility to make him feel better.

But shit, I've really trod on a nerve. I sort of thought he'd tell me he was a spy or a travel writer. He's staying in this suite twice the size of the room Liam and I are sharing, and as far as I can tell, he's all by himself, despite the shiny wedding band on his finger and—

Oh shit.

I grab a box of tissues from the night table and hand it to

him. He takes like six and buries his face into them as I stand awkwardly for a minute, trying to decide if I should leave or call down to guest services to see if there is an onboard therapist who deals with stuff like—

Stuff like—

Finally, I just *sit* awkwardly next to him, because it's at least better than standing, and—still awkwardly—pat his heaving back as he blows his nose and makes little snuffling gasps.

"I'm sorry," he says, wiping his eyes with the backs of his hands.

"No, hey, it's cool. I really shouldn't have asked."

"No. No. It's a fair question. Probably really does look weird that I'm in this great big room and—" The last words go high and squeaky, and he bites his lip while his chin wobbles under his beard.

"Oh, honey," I say, even though we are not nearly friendly enough for that, and the word makes him flinch, so I scoot a bit to give him some space. "Maybe you could answer some yes or no questions?"

The tissues are wadded up in his fists, and his gaze is on the carpet in front of him, but he nods.

"Okay, so you said yesterday you had a husband?"

He shakes his head.

"Fiancé?"

There's a pause, then a slow rippling shrug.

Jesus, I've really fubared this. "Is this supposed to be your honeymoon?"

A nod.

"But you're on your own?"

Another nod. More chin wobbling.

"Was your fiancé tragically crushed to death by a suspiciously convenient wildebeest stampede?"

That gets a tentative smile at least. "No," he croaks.

"He got called on a top-secret mission and had to leave

before the wedding to go save a flotilla of nuns and children adrift in the North Sea?"

"If it was top secret, how would I know about the nuns and children?" His smile is a little stronger, and his expression is so open I want to squeeze him and tell him everything will be okay.

"Did he—"

"He didn't show and sent me a text fourteen minutes later." He reaches into his pocket and thumbs through his phone before he flips it around and holds it towards me. The name Calvin is written at the top of the screen.

The last few messages read like this:

Doug: All checked in to the hotel. Think I forgot my toothbrush charger.

Calvin: We'll buy one in Florida. It's Miami, not the moon.

Doug: I'll see you tomorrow. I'll be the one in the front wearing the navy suit.

Calvin: Can't wait. Love you.

Doug: Love you too.

Then there's a gap, like the phone wants me to know time has passed between the messages. And then one more text from Calvin.

Calvin: Never mind. I'm sorry.

What the fuck? Never mind? "Never mind!" Even though I've never met this fucker, I'm immediately outraged on Doug's behalf.

"It's weird, right?"

"Never mind? Never mind is not the thing you say when you call off a wedding."

"That's what I thought." His smile is a little stronger.

"You tell someone *never mind* when you can't find your glasses and ask for help, but then realize as soon as you ask that they're on top of your head." I'm so mad I have to stand up and pace. "You don't say it when you realize the wedding isn't going to happen. What kind of asshole does that?"

His face starts to crumple again. I shove the tissue box at him once more, but my anger blows away, and I sink back down and let this poor, sad man I hardly know rest his head on my shoulder while he cries. My sleeve is wet by the time he sits up again, which is fine, because there's still a crusty streak of pink on my chest from the sapphic daiquiris the day before too.

"Sorry," he says again.

"Why the hell are you apologizing? You are not responsible for the shitty way people treat you." From my mouth to Doug's ears. God. I should really go tell Liam how lucky he is that I've put up with his bullshit and then push him over the rail.

Doug's phone chimes, and it's so sudden that he drops it.

"Shit." He reaches down to get it, and the hem of his shirt rides up, revealing a crescent moon of soft hairy back. He's not so fuzzy you could turn him into a rug, but I like a guy who doesn't manscape himself bald.

And shit, why am I thinking about him like that? He literally just had his heart pureed, and my boyfriend—even though I'm increasingly unsure he wants the title—is two floors down in the business centre.

"That's, uh—" He wiggles his phone in my direction. "There's a meet and greet with the captain for suite-class passengers. I should probably go check it out." He swallows hard, and suddenly I think about him last night, by himself at the mixer, and again sitting solo at dinner.

Fuck, this has to be miserable for him.

"I could go with you?" I offer.

He shakes his head. "No. That's okay. You've done a lot already."

"I made you cry!"

He gives me a lopsided smile. A small scar tugs at the edge of one dimple. "Calvin made me cry. You at least tried to make me feel better."

Watching him pull himself back together is painful, but he does it.

"Thanks." He puts on a brave smile.

I don't really want to go, but whether he's actually going to this captain thing or he just needs some space to fall to pieces again in private, he clearly wants me to leave. "I'm just down the hall if you need anything."

"Yeah, it's the door with the dick print on it, I remember." And then his face goes the colour of red wine as he gasps and slaps a hand to his mouth. His eyes are so wide they'll pop out of his head in another minute.

I laugh. I can't help myself. Here I am prying into his personal life, and he has the good manners to not remind me that he knows what every inch of my naked body looks like, even though he doesn't even know my last name.

But I have slept with men who knew even less.

Shit. I'm not thinking like that. Dougie Dougster does not need that from me right now. Not while his tears are literally still drying on my sleeve.

It's probably telling that *and I have a boyfriend* hardly registers in my reasoning.

"I'm so sorry. I don't know why I said that," he says, but I wave him off.

"I'll see you around."

Liam's not in our room. I do a loop of the ship. There's lots going on. The casino is busy, the main dining hall is full of parents and children in bathing suits, and some kind of art auction is going on in the central foyer. On the uppermost deck, there's a yoga class.

And the whole time I'm walking, it's like I'm slowly being reeled in, towards the business center, to have the conversation I was too stubborn to have last week, and last month, and—

He's sitting at a computer with a set of earbuds in.

"Mae? Mae, can you hear me?"

I shudder to think how much it must be costing him to try to Skype with someone.

"Mae?"

I settle into the chair next to him and log in, giving the computer my room number and name so they know who to charge this expense to. I keep my face politely blank while Liam tries over and over again to get a call to connect.

"Mae!"

I write an email to Pierce. He has never liked Liam and told me in no uncertain terms at Thanksgiving that a trip like this was not going to save our relationship—mostly because we don't really have a relationship. We have a mutually acceptable arrangement made up of great sex and a willingness to be each other's plus one at various functions. Living together just made economic sense in Vancouver's obscene real estate market. Somehow, I thought that was enough.

Dear P,

I was wrong. You were right.

T

I almost write *never mind*, because those two words are seared inside my brain. What a fucker. I don't know the ins and outs of Doug and Calvin's relationship, but the devastation on Doug's face makes it pretty clear—unlike Liam and I, who are both equally responsible for the situation we now find ourselves in—he had no idea about what was coming.

I hit send and ignore the immediate mental image that follows of Pierce's smug satisfaction. He argued long and hard that if I wanted to get away, I should dump Liam's ass, and then Pierce and I could go on a cruise to celebrate my liberation.

"Liam, we need to talk." I say.

"Give me a minute. I can't hear Mae."

"This isn't working." I don't feel sad when I say it. Frustrated. Tired. Embarrassed that I thought a vacation would fix all the reasons we aren't good together.

"You're right," he says, and I let out a long, relieved breath. Except then, Liam says, "The connection speed here sucks," as he angrily clicks his mouse.

The last thing I want is another public fight. As far as I'm concerned, we're done. If Liam wants to hash it out later—if he can unplug himself long enough to do so—we can, but I know the mistakes I've made. They're the same ones I always make. I build up the relationship in my head, create the narrative where I've finally met the perfect guy, and ignore every single red flag that says he isn't. Maybe once I thought I was in love with this man, but I've been kidding myself for months.

I go down to the shopping concourse, already feeling better. Time to move on. There are shops selling diamond rings and thousand-dollar watches, but towards the back I find a store clearly set up for the poor souls who arrive on their vacation only to realize their bathing suits are still in a dresser drawer or —like mine—in the airline ether where lost bags go.

My suitcase should be here tomorrow, but I'm on a cruise with exactly one of everything and nothing to swim in, so I don't even look at the price tags as I grab a pair of trunks off the shelf, along with a fresh T-shirt. I change quickly in my room, make a short call to guest services, and head to the pool.

Turns out the pool is jammed. Well . . . all the pools are jammed. The *Tropical Vista* has three. One for families, where children in brightly coloured inner tubes are running and jumping—and *screaming*. Holy Moses, why are small people so loud? Then there's an indoor atrium pool, which seems to mostly be for the most senior of the senior passengers and people who could also just as easily be napping in their rooms.

The main pool probably has a bigger footprint than our town house in Vancouver and is lined by four rows of loungers, all occupied. After about ten minutes of circling and trying to look casual, I finally claim a spot, as a group of forty-something women in floppy hats and brightly coloured cover-ups clear out, chatting loudly about going for facials at the spa. I throw my towel on one of the chairs they left behind and spread out.

Skin cancer is bad. I know. But tanning, stretching your whole body out and letting the sun soak into every pore, is *amazing*. I live in a place where it rains 170 days a year—never mind the days where it technically doesn't rain but we also don't even get an hour of sunshine. Someday I will regret my life choices, but right now, lying in the hot sun and feeling the last of the damp finally dry out of my bones is just about the best thing ever.

I turn regularly, just to make sure I don't burn on my first day, and trade watching seats with neighbors who want to go for a swim or grab a drink. All in all, it's a nice way to spend a day.

Not long after noon, I'm toasty and a little hungry. I'm standing at the bar because they're doing this amazing thing with fresh coconuts and those tiny bottles of rum or tequila like they serve on airplanes. The line is long, but I'm—finally—in that warm relaxed place I had hoped to find when I suggested this trip. I didn't realize finding it would require me to stop trying to get my boyfriend's attention when he's clearly more in love with his work than with me, but whatever. I've figured it out now, and life is good.

As the line crawls ahead, I scan the assembled crowds. So many people. But everyone is smiling and having a good time, and it strikes me that—out here anyway—everyone seems to know the people around them. No one out here is alone. Cruises are not meant to be done alone.

And so, of course, that's when I spot Doug.

He's in one of the hot tubs tucked behind the round poolside bar. He looks adorably awkward, if I'm being honest. His skin is pasty and flushed from the steam, and his short hair has gone spiky at the edges where it's wet. He's almost up to his chin in the water, which is funny, because he's not a short guy, and everyone else is only in water up to their chest. I wonder if he's self-conscious about his body. I love his shape. His torso was round and sturdy in his T-shirt this morning, and I love it when a guy like that wraps himself around me.

I shiver and look away, because I'm not supposed to be perving on poor heartbroken Dougie. If I want to find a cute cub to help me get over my breakup with Liam—which technically hasn't happened yet, but I think we can all agree this cruise is rapidly becoming a very expensive life lesson—when I get home, I can do that. But it won't be Doug. I should steer clear of him and let him heal.

Except, as the line keeps shuffling forwards—these drunken coconuts better be fucking magical—the woman sitting next to Doug in the hot tub starts to creep closer to him. She's got to be at least in her late seventies, if not her eighties. Her grey hair is all frizzy in the humidity and she's wearing a purple bathing suit with neon-coloured macaws printed on it. And the longer she talks, the lower Doug sinks in the water, until it's lapping at his nose, and she doesn't seem to notice at all. She just keeps talking to him with an animated smile. When I'm second in line, she pulls out her phone and starts scrolling through something, showing it to Doug, who keeps nodding politely, while everything about his body language screams "Get me out of here!"

Except that fucker Calvin said, "Never mind," and now Doug has no one to save him.

I get to the front of the line, and the bartender asks what I'll have. Screw the mystical coconut. They're going to be fussy for what I have to do next.

"Two piña coladas with an extra umbrella in each please."

The glasses are tall and frosty. I thank the bartender and march across the deck.

If Doug sinks any lower, he'll drown himself. The woman is still talking. With my biggest smile, I swing one leg over the edge of the hot tub and plop myself down with my most aggrieved sigh while I juggle the two drinks.

"Oh my God. That line was a nightmare."

Doug has popped back out of the water like a wide-eyed cork.

"You—" he starts to say, and he's about to give the game away, so I do the only thing I can think to do.

I shove the two piña coladas at him, and when his attention and hands are occupied, I haul him in for a kiss.

5

DOUG

The woman in the hot tub is named Myrna. She and her husband, Winston, are from Ocala, Florida. They take three cruises every year because, as Myrna puts it, "We just can't handle the cold anymore."

Before I can point out I'm from Toronto, where we use words like *polar vortex* and *Tuesday* synonymously, Myrna launches into her life story. She and Winston met in high school. She raised their kids while Winston worked as an oral surgeon.

When she starts showing me pictures of her grandchildren, all of whom are adults, and giving me a pointed arched eyebrow as she tells me which of those grandkids are unmarried, I know I'm screwed.

"And this is Molly. She's a dental hygienist. Single too." She gives me a wink.

Oh my God, somebody save me.

Only I'm seated as far away from the stairs as I can be, and I can't think of a polite way to leave. I'm not meeting anyone. Won't conveniently see anyone I know. When we go out, Calvin is the one who makes small talk. Now I'm trapped here with Matchmaking Myrna who thinks I'm straight and won't stop until I am betrothed to one of her lineage.

Except then a long, tanned leg splashes over the side of the hot tub without so much as a "hi, how are ya?" and the next thing I know I'm holding two frozen drinks and kissing Tripp.

Or he's kissing me.

No. Nope. I am kissing him back. His hands are on the sides of my face, and his lips are moving and so are mine, like they have a mind of their own, because my brain has completely shut down to the most basic primitive level.

He tastes like pineapples and rum and coconut. His lips are soft, but they kiss like they know what they're doing, which makes one of us at least. And just as I think he's about to pull away, he does this thing with his tongue along the seam of my mouth that makes me dizzy before he finally sits back, taking his drink from me. He gives the straw a long slurp while he watches me with mischief in his eyes. Then he smacks his lips and reaches around me, and only then do I remember Myrna is there, except, where before she was too happy to dominate the conversation, now she is staring at us with an open mouth and flushed cheeks that don't have anything to do with the hot tub.

"Hi," Tripp says. "I'm Doug's husband."

I nearly drop my piña colada.

"Oh. Hello." Myrna sounds decidedly less delighted to make Tripp's acquaintance than she did to make mine not that long ago.

When he's done shaking her hand, he shifts his drink and then drapes his free arm over my shoulder, pulling me close and kissing my temple.

"Missed you," he says. "Did you miss me?"

I give him a nervous smile, then, as he waggles his eyebrows, lean over to kiss his cheek. I mostly miss and get his ear, but don't have time to correct before frozen rum beverage is dribbling over my hand and towards the swirling water of the hot tub, which definitely can't be sanitary.

"Oh, there's Winston. Excuse me." Myrna wades over to the

stairs and exits without so much as a backwards glance. Whether she's disgusted by our sweet gay affection or already scripting how she'll break the news to dental hygienist Molly that she had me in her clutches and then I slipped away, I don't know, but I can't say I'm sorry to see her go.

Tripp's arm is still around me, and he laughs, waving from my shoulder. He squeezes me, making me bobble my drink some more, but he doesn't seem to care. "That was amazing!"

I gulp down a huge mouthful of piña colada, ignoring the stink eye from the other people around us for fouling their soak. The ice crystals go directly from my mouth to my sinuses, and I wince as the brain freeze darkens my vision.

"Oh, sugar bear," Tripp croons. "Are you okay?"

"Sugar bear?" I open one eye and then the other. His smile is blinding.

"I was trying it out. You don't like it?" He turns to the others in the hot tub. "Newlyweds. We're still working on pet names. It's been quite the whirlwind. We only met this summer." Tripp cuddles up against me, resting his head on my shoulder, no doubt gazing up at me adoringly. "But when you know, you know. Right, muffin top?"

Muffin top? Is that a joke about my weight? Look, not all of us can be rocking the slim-fitting trunks I caught a split-second glimpse of before Tripp settled himself in the hot tub, dashing poor Myrna and Molly's hopes.

Before I can protest, though, Tripp links his fingers between mine and kisses the back of my hand, right by the wedding band I still haven't taken off. Should never have put it on, but—in that moment after the chapel had emptied and I'd been left, literally standing at the altar while my mom and sisters formed a small circle not too far away and whispered urgently to each other—I wanted to know what it looked like.

The ring was my dad's: a fat gold band I had resized and cleaned until it shined like new. Inside it are my parents' initials and their wedding date. After we got back from the cruise, I'd planned to have mine and Calvin's engraved on the other side.

Good thing I didn't get it done in advance.

I haven't cried in almost three hours. Probably time to get started on that again. Except Tripp must see the distress on my face, because his hand tightens around mine and he says, "Ready for lunch?"

Lunch? I glance around, but there isn't a clock anywhere in my line of sight. What time is it? The thing with the captain was a bit of a bust. Me and a bunch of septuagenarians—mostly French Canadians—drinking mimosas while a man in a white uniform made a short speech, waved like he was boarding Air Force One, then went back through a small *Staff Only* door and we were left to chat.

"Come on." Tripp stands, water dripping from his shorts and down his legs. They're good legs. Strong, with swirls of dark blond hair. I stare longer than strictly appropriate, until I remember I'm supposed to be a newlywed who has known my husband for less than six months. I can stare all I want.

I gather up my towel, T-shirt, and hat from the lounger where I left them. Tripp has grabbed a fresh towel from the stacks that seem to be available everywhere and is mopping off his chest. I let myself look a little more. I mean, I've seen everything, but you're not supposed to ogle a helpless naked man in an awkward situation.

Your husband though . . .

Except he's not my husband. My husband is an ocean away in Toronto, doing God knows what, but he's not here. And he's not my husband.

"Doug Freeman, will you marry me"?

But he also said, "Oh my God, I can't wait for this wedding to be over so we can get on with our lives."

I don't know what my life is going to be like now. Calvin has been my rock for nearly three years.

"Okay!" Tripp's got his arm over my shoulders again, like it's meant to be there. "What do you feel like eating?"

"You don't have to eat with me. I mean, if you've got somewhere to be. Or someone to meet."

He snorts. "Liam? He is definitely not expecting me back. I don't even think he'll notice. They'll probably have to force him away from his computer to eat something later this evening."

"What's he even doing here?"

Tripp's face sobers. "That was my fault. I misjudged how broken our relationship was." He squeezes my shoulder. "One sec. Let me go get my shirt. It's over by the pool."

Was that what I did? Misjudged our relationship? Missed the signs?

I suck hard on my straw, eyes scanning the crowds for Tripp, until I see him coming back towards me, now in a neon-pink Tropical Vista T-shirt.

"Feel like sushi?" he asks with a smile. "There's an outdoor sushi place on the deck upstairs."

I wrinkle my nose. "I'm more of a cheese pizza kind of guy."

He gasps. "Sugar plum! Don't say things like that!"

I roll my eyes. "You can stop with the pet names. No one's going to hear them."

Tripp links an arm through mine and starts walking to the staircase to the upper deck. "Didn't Rat Bastard have pet names for you?"

"His name is Calvin," I say defensively. "And he—" He what? Told me once that pet names were childish and then only ever used them when he was talking to me like a child?

Sweetie, if you don't get more adventurous in your food choices, how can we ever have friends over?

We had friends over. Backyard barbecues, Raptors playoffs. And yeah, the food wasn't fancy—not like the five-course dinner parties Calvin wanted to throw—but everyone loves my home-made burgers.

Except maybe Calvin?

What if Calvin didn't like my burgers and never told me? I missed the part where he decided he didn't want to marry me, after all, so God only knows what smaller details I didn't catch.

"You okay?" Tripp's watching me with a frown.

I square my shoulders. "I'm fine. Let's have some sushi."

Sushi is . . . yeah, it's not really my thing. Tripp says to order some California rolls and tuna rolls. The tuna rolls are okay. They mostly taste like salty rice, maybe a little squishy in the centre. The California rolls, though . . . I should have told him I don't like avocado either.

But the piña coladas are amazing. Our drinks are half-done by the time we sit down, and high noon on the top deck of a cruise ship in the middle of the ocean is just about as far away as we can get from shade, so when the server asks if we'd like another round and Tripp raises an eyebrow, who am I to argue?

"I don't really like coconut," I say as I push my straw around the bottom of my glass, trying to find the last dregs of my second drink. "But these are pretty awesome."

"How can you not like coconut?"

I suck long and hard, until there's nothing but tropical-scented air left in my glass. "It gets stuck in your teeth and your gums. You're literally finding it twenty-four hours later, floating around in your saliva, even if you brush. But these . . ." I wiggle my glass. "They fixed that problem. No floaty bits."

Speaking of floating, what the piña coladas lack in unpleasant coconut texture, they make up for in rum. After two of them, not to mention the mimosas earlier, I'm bobbing nicely, even though you can't feel the motion of the ship at all, even this high up. I tilt my head back to face the sun and sigh heavily.

"Is that a happy sigh or a sad sigh?" Tripp asks. I glance at him, and he's got his straw between his teeth while he smiles at me. It's a fun smile. A nice smile. He's a nice guy. He's been the best part of the last seventy-two hours, and all he's done is flash

me, come over for coffee, and rescue me from aspiring grand-
mothers-in-law.

"Full sigh." The sushi isn't something I'll be rushing out for
when I get home, but it was fine, and then they brought these
bowls of green ice cream that were delish. On top of the drinks
and the giant breakfast from this morning, I probably don't need
to eat again for a week.

*"Honey, are you sure you weren't sucking in when they took your
measurements last time?"*

"Doug, you're wasting away. Please, you have to eat."

The server comes to our table and asks, "Can I have one of
your ship passes to charge your room?"

Tripp and I glance at each other. We hadn't discussed who
was paying for lunch. But I throw my card down on the table
before he can.

"For Myrna," I say.

He grins but doesn't argue. His eyes sparkle as he watches
me. The tip of his nose and his ears are turning pink, and I want
to tell him I have sunscreen, but I also don't want to sound like
his mother. And, since I've seen his pale ass, I know how tanned
he is, which means he probably knows exactly how much sun
he can take.

He's still watching me. His lips are pressed together, but the
corners are stretching wider and wider the longer we sit there in
silence.

"What?" I say.

The smile extends for a moment more before he says, "We
should get married."

6

TRIPP

Over the course of our lunch, I make a list of things that are just adorable about Doug. I'm not supposed to be attracted to him, but some of his mannerisms are objectively and undeniably the sweetest.

1) The way he smooths his napkin over his lap like we're at a fancy restaurant, when we're actually sitting at an overpriced outdoor sushi bar wearing our swim trunks and T-shirts and smelling like chlorine.

2) The meticulous way he unrolls the California rolls, scrapes out all the avocado, and then rolls the whole thing back up before nibbling on it, testing for any avo residue.

3) The intensity with which he sucks every single drop out of his piña colada, like a cartoon aardvark hunting for the very last ant. If I were allowed to be attracted to him, there are some very specific things I can think to do with a mouth like that.

4) How his whole being, from his face to his shoulders to his fucking aura, freezes when I say we should get married.

Good thing he's finished his drink. The straw is still between his lips, and if there were anything left, his shocked inhale would have rocketed it up the back of his throat, through his nose, and back out again. I would have inadvertently turned him into a Dougie fountain, and that would very decidedly not be adorable.

"M-married?" he stammers, eyes still huge.

"Well," I say, leaning back, letting him get used to the idea. "Not *married* married. But, you know. You're here by yourself. I'm basically here by myself. To keep up our morale and protect us from marauding Myrnas, we should keep up the whole husbands thing. I think it would be good for both of us."

"Marauding Myrnas . . . " His voice and his gaze get this faraway quality. There's a smear of piña colada—or maybe it's ice cream—in the corner of his beard, and I want to wipe it away. Or maybe kiss it off. Poor Dougie Dougster. If he were anyone else, I'd tell him we should be fuck buddies for the duration of this trip, but somehow, I don't think he'd agree to that. He seems like a real *no kissing until the third date* kind of guy, and I can respect that, especially given where he's at with his love life

"You need a wingman," I say. "I happen to be an excellent wingman. All my friends say so."

Actually, no one says that. Pierce says I suffer from SMD—Serial Monogamy Disorder. He says I hop from boyfriend to boyfriend and think every single one of them is the future Mr. Tripp, only to be disappointed when they don't live up to my dreamy expectations.

Case in point: Liam. Why did I ever think that was going to work?

As Pierce sees it, I'm never single long enough to be anyone's wingman, because I'm always in the throes of moony-eyed new love whenever he needs backup to go clubbing.

Except for right now. I am newly single—well, single enough. I have no idea if Liam heard anything I said in the business centre, but that is not my problem—Dougie needs cheering up, and who am I going to meet in the next seven days who needs me more than him?

He's rolling the glass gently between his palms, and his gaze is hopping from the table to the rail to the big ship's funnel and back again without ever landing on my face.

"I don't know," he says as he sucks on his lower lip, probably without even realizing he's doing it.

So. Fucking. Adorable.

"Trust me," I say.

"What about your boyfriend?"

And yeah, Doug doesn't know that I'm already over Liam. We had no business coming on this cruise in the first place. I'm sure he thinks every single other person on this ship is in a deeply loving and committed monogamous relationship, just to remind him how much he isn't right now. But he heard our fight this morning. Saw us at dinner last night.

"Let's just say Liam and I are about to take very separate vacations. And I'm not looking to start something new. Time for a hiatus."

"A hiatus?" Doug still doesn't look convinced.

"We'd be totally platonic. Think of it like a concierge-level travel buddy. You get someone to share meals with, hang out with, while being confident I am a hundred percent invested in making sure you have a good time."

His face scrunches up as he considers this. "But . . . why? Why would you do this for me?"

I'm pretty sure if I say anything that sounds remotely like I feel sorry for him—let's face it, though, how can I not?—he'll shut me down and probably never speak to me again. I'll have lost one real boyfriend and one fake husband in less than twenty-four hours. So instead, I say, "Because I owe you."

"You do?"

"Yeah." I give him my most charming smile. Nine out of ten guys who get this smile wind up coming home with me. "It takes a special kind of someone to rescue a naked stranger and not make it weird. Just imagine what would have happened if poor Myrna had found me."

He laughs. It's a soft sound. I want to roll in it like a pig in mud. "That's true, I guess."

"So, what do you say? Can I be Mr. Doug for the rest of this trip? No funny business. Just you and me keeping each other company and the busybodies at bay."

"Freeman."

I'm so deep into my sales pitch that I can practically hear the record scratch in my head. "What?"

"My last name is Freeman. Not Doug."

"Aw, Dougie. Are you asking me to change my name for you?" I roll it around in my brain, trying it on for size. Tripp Freeman. Sounds like I've fallen down the stairs and don't know how to stop, but I kind of like it.

He's still tonguing his straw. The real Mr. Freeman has a serious oral fixation that I am most definitely not going to take advantage of, because I am a gentleman.

"Okay," he says.

My heart quite literally skips a beat. I didn't realize how much I wanted him to say yes.

"Yeah?" I'm smiling and I can't stop. Spending a few days being Doug's husband will be fun!

———

We pass most of the afternoon by the pool. Doug goes back to his suite for a bit and returns with a tablet. He's a reader, my new husband, but when I ask him what he's reading, he gets this nervous look on his face and holds the iPad closer to his chest. But I only need a little wheedling to get him to fess up that he's reading some kind of high fantasy thing with elves and wizards.

"Why would you be embarrassed about that?" I ask.

His expression gets tight, his mouth curling under itself while two spots of colour spill over his cheeks. I'm learning this is how his face works when he thinks about Mr. Dickhead

Fiancé, but I don't want to make him sadder, so I say, "I'm not much of a reader. My favourite thing to read right now is this queer web comic set in outer space."

He glances at me, still a little nervous that I might be fucking with him, but when I ask him again what the book is about, he explains it to me in excruciating detail. It's kind of boring. Maybe you have to read it. It involves a lot of magic, and elves, and a quest to find a thing that sounds pretty impossible, but his whole face lights up as he speaks, and that's good enough for me.

I finally do get one of those drunken coconut things, and holy smokes it really is amazing. I offer one to Doug, but piña colada seems to be as close as he'll get to actual coconut, and he settles for a banana daiquiri instead.

Around midafternoon, full of sun and rum, I doze off on the lounger. Doug is still reading beside me, fully engrossed in his screen. I wake up when someone drapes a towel over my back.

"I don't want you to burn," he says, and I drift off, happy at that brief moment of caring. If he's looking out for me, he can't be sad all the time, and the thought leaves me with a buzz of accomplishment.

The happy feeling lasts through dinner. Doug orders the Caesar salad and the chicken, and I pretend not to notice how he makes sure the gravy never touches his green beans. The motion is precise, practiced, and the way he—every few bites— uses his knife to push back the gravy tide as it creeps across his plate says he's done this before. I think about the way he didn't want to tell me about his book and wonder if—here too, with his eating habits—the Incredible Disappearing Fiancé gave him a hard time.

Why would Doug be with someone like that?

Then again, I've just wasted a year of my life with Liam the Workaholic by telling myself I enjoyed being with someone who let me maintain my independence, when I'm not even sure he knew I was there half the time, so what do I know?

We walk back to our floor. Doug looks thoughtful as we stop at my door.

"Is this the part where I kiss you goodnight?" His shy smile makes my toes curl.

So a-fucking-dorable.

"I don't kiss until the third date."

He nods, like he expected that, and I'm almost sad he doesn't push it, before I remember I'm his wingman and not his husband or boyfriend or anything else that actually merits a kiss.

"Do you want to come to my place for breakfast?" he asks.

"I'm not really much of a breakfast eater." Or a morning person, but when his smile fades, I quickly say, "But I'll come for coffee."

That shores his smile up, and he says. "Good! Eight o'clock?"

"Eight o'clock?" I squawk. "I thought this was supposed to be a vacation."

"We have to be on the wharf for the tequila tasting at nine."

I grin. He's got the whole trip planned out, and all the excursion tickets are paid for, so why not go? It's what a good husband would do.

"Okay." I roll my eyes, but he smiles. "I'll see you at eight."

My happiness bubbles just long enough for me to enter my room, where it promptly bursts because Liam is there.

He's sitting on the bed. A mountain of papers is strewn over the sheets, and two plates of food, along with two overturned stainless-steel covers, are on the coffee table, which he has dragged closer so he can eat while he works.

But his eyes widen when he sees me, and he hurriedly scrambles to pick up all the papers. "Hey, you're back. I went down to the dining room, but I didn't see you."

I wasn't in the dining room. Doug had a reservation at one of the specialty restaurants, because he seems to have booked everything in advance. It was tasty too. He may have stuck to the chicken and beans, but I had grilled swordfish and some kind of squash puree that was to die for.

"Did you get a hold of Mae?" I slide onto the couch.

"Yeah."

"And?"

He cocks his head to one side. "Do you really want to hear about that?"

"No." I fold my arms over my chest.

"Should we talk about this?" He gestures to the bed where all his things are piled, and the one that is now next to it. Earlier, I called guest services and told them to separate our beds. What looked like a smallish queen-size bed is actually two smaller singles pushed together, with a mattress pad on top. Liam and I are stuck on this boat together for six more days, but I do not want him to get the wrong idea.

"What's there to talk about?"

He gives me a lazy smile. My smile may be ninety percent effective in bringing home the next new love of my life, but his has always been my kryptonite.

Though not anymore.

"I missed you today," he says, his eyelids going heavy, the way they do when he's turned on.

"You missed me?" My stomach gurgles the way *it* does when I'm nauseous.

"Yeah." He undoes the top two buttons of his shirt. "I'm sorry. I haven't been a very good boyfriend these last couple days."

Jesus, he really didn't hear a single thing I said at the business centre this morning, did he? "Do you honestly think you have any chance of getting laid right now?"

"Tripp." He pouts. "I'm sorry. I got freaked out at the idea of being disconnected from work."

"The whole point of coming here was to be disconnected from work!" I shouldn't have said it like that, because it's the same argument we've been having for months and makes it sound like I still want to work through this.

He proves my point as he gets up on his knees and says, "I know. I'm sorry. I'll do better. Tomorrow, I'm all yours."

My throat tightens. I don't want him tomorrow. Or ever. Not anymore. And it's not even that I had a nice day with Doug. That's something different. But Liam and I . . . "We aren't good together. You and me. We don't work."

He arches an eyebrow. "Sure we do."

"No, we don't. You know we don't."

He gets off the bed, walking towards me. "What are you talking about?"

"We aren't boyfriends," I say. "Not really. We're just fuck buddies who happen to live together."

Liam's mouth curves into an amused smile, and he puts his hands on my hips, pulling me towards him. "We like our space. What's so wrong with that?"

We've done this dance before, so I can't blame him for misunderstanding. Usually, when we fight, it ends in messy make-up sex, but lately that routine has been getting stale. Orgasms don't actually constitute a behavior change.

But apparently I'm the only one who thinks so. "Tripp. Let me make it up to you."

He bends his head to kiss me, but I shove him away, falling backwards onto the couch again. "Stop!"

He looks confused for a second before realization finally seems to dawn. "Are you breaking up with me?"

I wipe my mouth with the back of my hand, even though he didn't actually kiss me. "I broke up with you this morning. Not my fault you didn't notice."

"Well, what the fuck!" His hands ball up, and his jaw tightens. "I thought this was what you wanted? I thought we agreed we weren't going to be the kind of couple who lived in each other's pockets."

"We aren't a couple. We're friends with benefits who are only friends to share the cost of rent."

He scoffs. "Don't be so dramatic."

"I'm not dramatic. I'm telling you I'm done pretending that we care about each other."

"I care about you." Hurt flashes in his eyes for a second, prompting an echo of guilt inside me, but I ignore it.

"Not as much as you care about work. About the label. And Mae. I'm done making excuses. I'm not eating alone anymore."

"Tripp." He holds a hand out to me, but I stay where I am. If I take it, he'll think I'm caving. He'll try to take me to the bed so he can say he's sorry, and touch me, and eventually fuck me until I'm screaming his name. It's how it's always worked between us before, and I'm suddenly ashamed at how shallow I've been to let myself be treated like that.

"No."

"You can't ask me to choose you over the label. That's my baby. My passion."

"I know." Some of my anger fades to sadness. I've always known I wasn't his priority, but I liked the idea of being the guy on his arm at parties and shows. "But I need to find someone who puts me first."

He laughs. Laughs! The fucker. "Is this what you spent all day doing? Working up this speech?"

I gape. Is that how little he actually thinks of me? "I didn't actually think you'd be here."

"Where the fuck else would I be?" His earlier softness is fading, giving way to anger. "We're on a boat in the middle of the ocean. Not many places to go."

"Well, you can have the business centre. We'll be in Mexico tomorrow. I'll entertain myself. We just need to be mature about this for a few more days."

"Mature?" He huffs. "You're the one who got all passive aggressive and split up the beds."

That wasn't passive aggressive, that was proactive. "Because I don't want to be your boyfriend anymore, Liam. This room is Switzerland until we get back to Florida. Otherwise, you do your thing, I'll do mine, and we never have to see each other again after we're home."

"Tripp."

"No." I'm not backing down on this. I should have made this decision ages ago. But tomorrow is a fresh start. Doug and I are going tequila tasting, and I am going to learn how to be someone's friend instead of falling into their bed the first time they smile at me.

Liam holds up his hands. "Fine. If that's what you want."

It's what he wants too. Liam's competitive. Driven. He doesn't like to lose, and I'm sure me pulling the plug on this relationship before he gets a chance is some kind of defeat for him. But when the dust has settled and I've moved out, I bet he won't even miss me.

I don't sleep well. The bed is narrower than a standard one and lumpy in weird places. Liam suddenly develops a snore, which is not something I've ever heard him do in the whole time we've been together.

But I must fall asleep, because the next thing I know, the too-chirpy *bong bong* is sounding on the PA system, but the morning announcements are interrupted by the sound of a heavy-duty zipper sliding shut.

I open my eyes, and Liam has his back to me. He's still in his collared shirt, and even though he's been wearing it for three days now, it's still unwrinkled.

The sound I've heard is him zipping his laptop case closed.

"What are you doing?" I ask, and then the last of the sleep clears and I remember yesterday.

"Mae emailed. There's a problem in Vietnam now. I have to

go home." He glances over his shoulder, giving me an apologetic smile he has never once given me before when work drags him away from whatever party, date, or make-out sesh we happened to be involved in.

That's how I know he's lying, and he's using work as an excuse to escape.

"You're flying back to Vancouver?" I ask, rubbing my eyes as I sit up.

"Already booked my flight."

I should feel something. Disappointment. Relief. I'm just numb. Sorry I've wasted so many days and nights chasing something and someone that was never really going to happen.

"Okay," I say. "I'll come get my stuff after the cruise is over."

"That's fine."

He's gone by the time I get out of the shower.

It's only as I'm putting yesterday's clothes back on that I remember Doug.

Who I promised to meet for coffee at eight.

And it's eight-thirty.

"Oh shit."

He probably thinks I've stood him up. I can picture his poor, splotchy, tear-stained face as I scramble into my clothes and make a dash for the hall, barely remembering to grab my key card off the dresser.

I spot the psychedelic leprechaun and bang on the door opposite, breathing hard.

He opens it, and I relax. No splotchy face. No suspicious eyes. He smiles and actually looks happy to see me.

"Sorry," I say. "Slept in."

He nods like he wasn't expecting anything more nefarious than that. "Come on in. We've got a few minutes before we have to go down." He leads the way to his balcony where a pretty selection of pastries and fruit is set up, along with the coffee pot and mugs. He's in a short-sleeved collared shirt and a pair of turquoise shorts. The shorts are seriously amazing. They show off his ass and calves spectacularly.

"Sleep okay?" he asks.

"Yeah." I nod, then wince as something pulls in my neck. "Not really. Liam and I broke up and slept in separate beds. The mattress was so narrow I could hardly move. Think I pinched something."

"I'm sorry about your boyfriend."

And I guess that is the appropriate response, but I'm already so over it. "It's fine."

"And about your neck. I totally would have brought my own pillow, but Cal—" He bites his lip, and I'm right back to where I was yesterday, thinking Doug is just the most adorable little butter tart ever. But he seems to be doing better today, because instead of crumpling, his smile brightens, and he motions towards the other chair on the balcony. "Have a seat."

I do, giving my head an experimental twist as I settle in. It only hurts when I turn to the left. I'll just have to keep Doug on my right side today.

I go to pour my coffee, and as the glorious brown brew hits the bottom of the mug, Doug squeaks. I freeze. "What?"

His face is splotchy now, but not from sadness. I think he might actually be blushing. But he says, "Look inside."

As I tip the mug, something slides against the porcelain. Frowning, I peer into it.

A shiny silver wedding band winks up at me.

7

DOUG

Bad idea. Oh God, what on earth was I thinking?

I'd had too much time to think, that's the problem. When Tripp didn't show up at eight for breakfast, I could feel the anxiety starting again. First Calvin, then Tripp. Never mind that one was a wedding and the other was coffee.

So, to keep myself calm, I went through the plan for today again. Off the boat at nine. Pickup at ten. Tour for three hours. Back to the boat by two. Boat leaves at four. I'd heard horror stories about people getting delayed on excursions and the boat leaving without them, so I made sure to pick tours that gave us lots of time to get back.

Once I'd reviewed all that, I started working in contingencies for what it would mean to have Tripp with me instead of Calvin. Would he be a shopper? Would he want to buy a bunch of souvenirs? We probably had time for that before we got back on the boat. I'd heard the cruise ports were basically prefab dives with the same stuff for sale at each stop, but that sometimes you could find neat places not too far away where they had local things and wouldn't gouge you—too much.

Maybe I could buy my mom and my sisters some jewelry. Earrings or a necklace.

My gaze dropped to my dad's ring, still on my hand, and a thought crossed my mind.

Now, horror slowly turns my insides to slime, as Tripp stares at the ring in the bottom of the coffee mug with an unfathomable expression on his face.

"Sorry, I—" I reach for the mug, but he tugs it away from me and tips it over, letting a trickle of coffee pour out before the ring tumbles onto the saucer with a clatter.

"This is—"

"A bad idea. I'm really sorry. Forget about it." I go to grab for it again, but he picks it up, pinched between two fingers, and holds it between us.

"Is this his?"

My eyes sting as I nod.

"And you want me to wear it?"

"Well, I was thinking . . . " What I'd been thinking was that while we were touring the tequila factory—brewery or maybe distillery?—we'd probably be with other people from the cruise, and we'd start chatting. Where are you from? Have you been on a cruise before? Oh, you're on your honeymoon! Isn't that romantic? And then Matchmaking Myrna or whoever we were talking with would glance down and see the big gold ring on my hand and Tripp's naked fingers, and they'd know.

Why I cared whether they knew didn't enter into it. I just couldn't handle any more humiliation.

Tripp bounces it in his hand a few times. I close my eyes as a vision plays in front of me—him missing and the ring tumbling from his palm, onto the balcony, under the rail, and out into the ocean.

"It doesn't weigh anything," he says.

"Titanium." Calvin had said gold rings were dated, and he didn't see the point in spending so much money on something he wouldn't wear anyway. I didn't understand why he didn't think he'd wear it. My dad wore his ring every day until cancer had eaten away so much of him the ring wouldn't stay on anymore. But picking a fight with Calvin about a ring when we had so many other decisions to make seemed petty.

Maybe if I'd done it, though, I would have seen sooner that he wasn't going to last.

And yet, while I've been rehashing the failure of our wedding—again—Tripp has slipped the ring over his finger and is holding it up in the sun.

My heart thumps as I stare at it, thinking about the way a wedding band is so significant while being so small. It's a single strip against the creases of his palm and the calluses on his fingers. Without it, how would anyone know he's mine?

Except he's not mine. This is just pretend. I swallow a mouthful of coffee and nearly scald my tongue.

"You okay?" His voice is deep and smooth. His eyes are really blue this morning. Dark blue, like the suit Calvin was wearing the first time I met him. But where Calvin's hair is so brown it's almost black, Tripp's is what my mom would call dirty blond. His features are sharp, his eyes a little too far back in his head to make him really handsome, but he's glancing from me to the ring and back in a way that makes my heart race.

His gaze drops, and he takes a piece of melon off the plate between us and pops it in his mouth. "Sorry," he says while he chews. "Should I take it off?"

"No!" I put my hand up to stop him as he wraps his fingers around his knuckle. "No, that's exactly what I wanted you to do. I just . . . " I didn't expect it to mean anything to me when he did. Calvin could decide he didn't want to wear it so easily. I thought everyone else would feel the same way.

He holds it back out, admiring it, and then smiles at me. "My last name is Gillingham, by the way."

I swallow a laugh. "Gillingham and Freeman? We're the WASPiest couple ever."

His grin spreads, and whatever happened between us about

the ring has passed. "We should probably change our names to Chet and Bryson, while we're adopting new surnames."

"Hello, I'm Chet Gillingham-Freeman."

Tripp's eyes go wide, and his mouth drops open. "Freeman-Gillingham, excuse you. And I wanted to be Chet."

"You look way more like a Bryson."

He shakes his head as he snorts, but before he can say anything, he's interrupted by the melodious *bong bong,* and the cruise director lets us know we can now disembark in Mexico.

I've never been to Mexico. Up until a few years ago, I'd never really been much of anywhere. After I got promoted at work, though, I started traveling more. Along with more local trips to Ottawa and Montreal, I went to film festivals in San Francisco, London, and even Lisbon.

Still, walking off the ship next to Tripp feels like being in a whole new world. The sky is blue, and all the buildings in the cruise port are made from a creamy-coloured concrete. Palm trees sway and a zillion tourists mill around, looking for guides holding up signs that say things like *Jeep Tour* and *Swim with Dolphins.*

"I've always wanted to do that," Tripp says, pointing at the dolphin sign. I wrinkle my nose, and he laughs. "What?"

"I looked into it. It didn't look super hygienic. You're in this pool with all these other people and the dolphins. The pictures made the water look kind of green. I think people imagine it's going to be in the ocean, and it's not."

He cocks his head. "I hadn't thought of it like that."

"Plus, I'm not a very good swimmer."

He nudges me and juts his chin towards an elderly woman with a cane, who is standing in line for the dolphin trip next to three very excited children who are probably her grandkids.

"If she can swim with the dolphins, I'm pretty sure you can too," he says.

My cheeks flush, and I glance away. I don't tell him I

kiddingly suggested the dolphin thing to Calvin at dinner one night and he rolled his eyes and called it tacky. It probably is, but everything around us is tacky, so now I'm not so sure why tequila is classier than dolphins.

We find the signpost for our tour. About twenty people are already there. A few couples, none of them same-sex, a few groups of women. Four guys in flip-flops and puka shell neck-laces who clearly don't believe in sunscreen are laughing way too loudly as they drink beers from plastic cups branded with the giant tiki hut-esque bar located near the beach.

Soon enough, an enthusiastic guide loads us onto a bus and launches into a history of Mexico as we roll down a busy city street.

Tripp nudges me. "I should probably have asked this before, but—"

"What?"

His smile is amused. "You're so jumpy. I just wanted to know if you have any traumatic tequila memories I should be aware of. You know, as your husband."

My cheeks flush with the way he rolls that last syllable around on his tongue. "I don't think so?"

He nods. "Trust me, you'd know. The last time I had tequila, I woke up naked in Stanley Park in the middle of Canada Day fireworks."

I snort. "I can see that."

"You can?" He frowns.

"Well, yeah," I say, pleased he hasn't caught on to my joke. "I mean, I have no trouble picturing you naked."

"Bitch!" He gasps and swats at my arm, and I laugh, squirming away from him, even though there's nowhere to go in the cozy bus seats. Tripp grins at me, tongue between his teeth. "Anyway. That was an extreme case. My twenty-second birthday, I think."

"Your birthday's in July?"

"June. The twenty-fifth. Yours?"

"April second."

He whistles. "Dodged the April Fool's bullet, did you?"

I groan. "Barely." Despite all my protests, my sisters took every opportunity to plan and execute elaborate birthday pranks the whole time I was growing up.

The bus rolls to a halt, and we all get off. The dude-bros are still loud and excited and carry on with a lot of backslapping about how long it's been since their last drink. I keep my distance. Sure, I'm an adult, and it's not like I really have anything to worry about from these guys, but people like them always make me a little nervous.

A hand at the small of my back nearly has me jumping out of my skin before I register Tripp's coconut and sunscreen scent "Easy there," he says.

I hold myself stiff for a second, waiting for someone to notice us or shuffle away like Myrna did in the hot tub, but everyone's attention is turned to our guide as he explains the finer points of agave cultivation.

The hand at my back stays there the whole time. It's warm, and my shirt starts to get sticky underneath it, but I don't mind. It's like it's holding me there. Anchoring me to the ground like very little has.

Flying to Miami by myself was one of the most disorienting things I'd ever done. I nearly missed my flight, even though my mom dropped me off three hours before the departure. I got turned around once I was through security and wound up at the wrong end of the terminal, sitting in the last row of seats with my headphones on and my head down. I had never wanted to disappear so much in my life.

I've flown by myself before for work. I know how to navigate an airport, but not when all I can do is replay that moment at the altar over and over. If I'd had someone—anyone—with me, to hold my hand or keep a steadying palm on me, I might have noticed I was in the wrong place before they'd put out the ominous "this is the final call for passenger Freeman . . ." announcement.

The horticultural lesson ends, and Tripp loops his elbow through mine as we're led into a tasting room.

"If I get wasted—" he says.

"I'll go look for you in Stanley Park."

He laughs, eyes crinkling at the corners, and the expression makes me ridiculously happy. I like that there are enough pieces of me holding together to make someone laugh. Doesn't hurt that Tripp's the one laughing either. Like his voice, it's a low sound that rumbles through his chest and hits me directly in my belly, making it go all quivery.

Did I ever feel the same when Calvin laughed? I hate how much I'm second-guessing everything now. So many of our years together were anything but funny. I don't know if the fact I can't really describe what Calvin sounds like when he laughs is a sign that we weren't well suited to each other or just another sign of the times, like the way we were on a first-name basis with every nurse in the pancreatic oncology ward at Princess Margaret.

We take seats at a round table with eight chairs. The remaining six get taken up by a man and woman and then another group of four women. The women are sisters, all from New Hampshire. They have names like Kirsten and Kendra. The couple are Tony and Grace from Camden, New Jersey.

"And you two are . . ." Grace says.

Before I can speak, Tripp puts an arm around my shoulder and says, "I'm Tripp, and this is my husband, Doug."

"Aww," one of the Ks says. "Husbands. That's so sweet. Have you been married long?"

Tripp squeezes me, which I take as the cue that it's my turn to say something, but I can barely tear my eyes off the tabletop, suddenly shy. "We're on our honeymoon."

More happy sighs from the sisters, while Tony and Grace

smile politely and Tripp waggles his borrowed wedding band for everyone to see. My hands twitch, fighting an anxious reflex to cover mine, because we suddenly seem to be the centre of a lot of attention.

"Where are you from?" Grace asks.

"Toronto," I say, at the same time Tripp says "Vancouver."

The happy interest stills, condensing into confusion as my cheeks go hot. I knew we shouldn't have done this. We didn't even attempt to create a plausible backstory.

I'm ready to bolt for the bus, but Tripp takes my hand and kisses the back of it, just below my wedding band. "Sorry." He rolls his eyes in self-deprecating amusement. "Toronto. I moved there right before the wedding. Still getting used to saying it out loud."

Grace smiles, perfectly accepting of his explanation. I start to relax as little sparks shoot up and down my spine while his thumb rubs back and forth over my ring. Except then Grace says, "And how did you meet?"

"We—" Tripp turns to me, lips puckered. I am going to be of no use to him on this because I can't lie to save my life. "We met—"

"Okay, everyone!" A new guide claps his hands, drawing our attention.

I have trouble concentrating while he speaks. Just like while I wandered the airport feeling like anyone who stopped to look at me knew I'd just had my heart ripped out, now I know that anyone—not even just the people sitting at our table—around us must know we're lying. That two days ago we were strangers and we're making shit up as we go along for my peace of mind and Tripp's amusement.

The guide tries to teach us the proper way to sniff a glass of tequila, but I'm so caught up, I inhale too much and the aroma burns all the way back to my sinuses. I cough reflexively while a few people giggle, and Tripp thumps my back and hands me glass of water.

"You okay, bumblebee?" he says.

I'm not. This thing with Tripp was supposed to be about helping me blend in, but two casual questions from people I've never met before and will probably never see again and I'm left feeling more exposed than ever.

"Sugar bear?" Tripp asks when I don't say anything. His mouth is close to my ear, and it makes the hairs on the back of my neck stand up.

"I'm okay," I say, taking another drink of water.

I never do learn the proper way to taste tequila. The guide talks about aromas and distillation, about why the stuff at the bar will give you a headache but the tequilas they serve here are just as good as any premium vodka or whisky. The words all go over my head, even as the tequila burns my throat.

After the tasting, we're led out to a sunny patio for lunch. Tripp and I stand in line, and I watch nervously as women in loose cotton blouses and flowery skirts ladle juicy meat and slimy green something onto little yellow tortillas.

"Those don't look like the tacos we have at home," I say, sounding like the worst kind of tourist. I may not have learned the refined art of sipping my tequila, but that doesn't mean my head isn't floating a little bit after the five glasses we were served, so keeping my mouth shut is a task.

"I'm sure you can ask for it without nopales," Tripp says behind me.

"The what?"

"It's cactus. Really yummy."

I wrinkle my nose, and when the woman putting the tacos together points at the nopales, I shake my head, feeling like the most spoiled child in the world for not eating what's on offer, but she doesn't give me a second glance, instead turning to smile enthusiastically at Tripp, who nods and says, "Con todo, por favor!"

"Chauplines?" she asks, pointing at a bunch of little plastic pouches stacked up to one side of the serving dishes. I peer at their contents. They sort of look like shrivelled cheezies, except redder.

"Si!" Tripp says excitedly and takes a bag.

We find a table, and Tripp goes to get us some drinks. I stare at our meal while he's gone. The green thing—the Naples or whatever—on his tacos looks squishy. I pick one up between my fingers and bite into it. It's . . . not awful. Bit slimy, but mostly doesn't taste like anything.

The little packet of orange cheesy things is on the table between my plate and Tripp's. Maybe I should try them too. Are they supposed to be some kind of topping? I like cheese on my tacos.

I open the top and pour a few into my hand. I know right away they're not cheese. Too light. Too crumbly.

Too many antennae and legs?

What the hell is this?

8

TRIPP

A while ago, I dated a Mexican tattoo artist. He was from Oaxaca. We only lasted a few months, but if I learned anything from him, it was this:

Cheddar cheese has no business on tacos.

The best cure for hangovers is posole—the hotter the better.

And, when the catastrophe hits and we no longer have farmland for livestock, humanity will survive on—

"It's grasshoppers!" Doug's voice echoes over the patio as I come back with our margaritas. He spins, looking for me, eyes wide like a child's. "Tripp! It's grasshoppers."

I can't help but smile, even as I half expect him to hop up and start dancing around like his chair is on fire. Instead, he keeps his eyes locked on me, his hand held out like he's holding a bomb.

"Did you try one?" I ask, setting his margarita in front of him before I take my seat across the table. I pick one off his palm and pop it into my mouth. "Tastes like barbecue chips."

"It does?"

"Yup." Only because they've been doused in salty barbecue seasoning. Otherwise, my experience with eating insects is they mostly don't taste like anything. "Go on, have one."

His eyes are like saucers as he glances between me and the dried grasshoppers. If he says no, I won't press. I bought them for fun, but Doug eating them or not isn't what I'm going to remember from this morning.

What I'm going to remember is the way he was tense through the whole tequila tasting, and I couldn't do anything to make it better.

He pinches a grasshopper between his fingers, eyeing it before he pops it into his mouth, chewing slowly.

"Well?" I say when he swallows.

"They're okay. Don't think I want more, though."

I'm super proud of him for even trying. To reward him, I cup his hand in mine and draw it towards me. Before he can ask what I'm doing, I drag my tongue over his palm, licking up the rest of our snack.

The expression on his face when I look up again is definitely the part I'm going to remember from this lunch.

He gapes at me for a minute while I swallow my chapulines and take a sip of my margarita. When I don't say anything, he picks up his taco, keeping his eyes on me the whole time he takes a bite.

"So, what was up with you before?" I ask as we eat.

I bought margaritas in souvenir glasses as big as our heads, and his voice is muffled from behind one. "When?" But the expression on his face as he sets the glass down says he knows exactly what I'm talking about.

"Before. Right when the tasting started." My blood burns when I say tasting. Doug's palm tasted like salt and lime, and I want to lick it again.

"Oh. That." He becomes very focused on his taco. "I don't think we can do this."

My burgeoning pride screeches to a halt. "Why not?"

"Because we don't know each other. It's impossible to put

together all the details of a long-term relationship. We don't even know where we live."

"Toronto. We settled that."

He sighs. "Tripp."

"What?"

His face gets pinched while he chews. He does get uptight when things aren't completely organized and planned.

I grab another handful of grasshoppers, grind them up between my palms, and sprinkle them on my taco. "What do you want to know?"

"Everything," he says. I laugh. Poor Dougster. Does he even guess how sweet he is?

I sigh and rattle off the facts I can think of off the top of my head. "I'm an only child. My parents are divorced. I grew up in Victoria and moved to the mainland to go to university. I have three degrees."

"Three degrees?" Doug asks, while his taco dribbles down his wrist. He sucks it off, and I can't help the way I shudder.

"I've got a bachelor's and master's in history, and another bachelor's in economics."

"Really?" His voice rises. "And what do you do for a living?"

"I run a doggie daycare."

He nearly drops his margarita.

I'm used to the reaction my career usually causes. Especially when Liam and I went places, because he always gives off this air of sophistication, and I inevitably wind up brushing dog hair off whatever I chose to wear. I love what I do, but know it seems a bit anachronistic with my swaths of education.

"I suppose people in Vancouver probably pay a lot for someone to look after their dogs."

"They do," I say slowly, because if I'm not careful, I'll start to have flashbacks of the fight I had with my dad when I told him I wouldn't be finishing my PhD, and reliving that won't be fair to Dougie. "But I do it because I love it. Dogs are easy. They have no pretence, so you never have to guess with dogs." As opposed to so many of my boyfriends who I thought were one thing and turned out to be something completely different.

"Do you have a dog?" Doug asks.

"Yeah." I pull out my phone, like the proud pet parent I am. "Trixie. She's a Shiba Inu mix."

He coos appropriately as I show him the pictures. The best way to a man's heart is to say nice things about his dog.

"What about you?" I ask when we're done ogling my baby. "What do you do for a living?"

He sits up and smiles. "I'm the programming director for Out & About. It's the biggest queer film festival in Canada."

"That is—" Like he must be regarding my canine career path, I'm surprised. If he'd asked me to guess, I would have said a teacher. Maybe an engineer. Something where he can think complex, technical thoughts or explain to other people how something works. But a gay film festival is— "That's pretty cool! How long have you done that?"

"My whole career. I started as a volunteer usher when I was in university, then got a job when I graduated. I guess you could say I worked my way up the ladder, except we're pretty far away from corporate."

"Programming director. Sounds pretty important."

He smiles shyly, and my chest warms at the sight of it. "I mean, I have a team; it isn't just me. We're in charge of choosing all the films that get shown at the festival, along with a smaller children's festival in the summer, and a couple other gala fundraising nights throughout the year. That's how I met Calvin, actually."

My next sip of margarita gets caught in my throat, and I cover my mouth to cough. Doug doesn't seem to notice, though, because he keeps talking.

"He's the senior vice president of partnerships at one of the banks. They love to sponsor events and organizations like ours.

He was at a gala one night. We were doing a Cary Grant tribute, and he was assigned to sit next to me."

"And he swept you off your feet?"

He smiles as he polishes off his margarita. "No. But he kept calling. Or stopping by, even when the thing we needed from the sponsorship team was way too menial for someone at his level. Took me a year to figure out he was interested in me." He hums a happy little tune and runs his finger around the last of the salt still stuck to his glass.

I'm not jealous. I'm not. What right do I have to be jealous when my fake husband wants to remember the happier moments of his beady-eyed ex-fiancé's—come on, you know he's beady-eyed—early days of wooing? If it helps him forget the awfulness that came at the end, who am I, of all people, to begrudge him that?

But I see the moment the awfulness comes back to him. No matter what came before, whether it was sweet or passionate, whether they were best friends or got off on making each other angry, the end is still the same.

"Sweetie pie," I say, trying to think of something to comfort him. That's my goal for the rest of this trip. To see that sad expression as little as possible.

A photographer appears. He doesn't speak much English but makes it clear he wants to take our picture. Doug tries to protest, but I hop around to his side of the table, squeezing against him.

"Come on, it'll be fun!" I lift my empty margarita glass and hold the pose until Doug finally does the same. I can't turn my head to check if he's smiling, so I do my best to smile for both of us. The shutter clicks, and the photographer tells us we can see the photos back on the ship.

"Everyone!" Our guide claps his hands. "It's time for the flyers!"

We're led to a small amphitheater with wooden benches. Doug and I sit together, and he holds himself stiffly beside me. I stretch out until my hand is braced on the far side of him, but he doesn't react, neither to lean in nor push me away.

The guide tells us about the tradition of the Papantla flyers and their rain dance. It sounds pretty magical as they begin their climb up the slender pole in the middle of the field. It must be at least twenty feet tall, and I have to squint into the bright blue sky as they go.

Doug gasps. "Are they going up there?"

"Yeah, weren't you listening?"

He shakes his head. "No, I was—" He trails off, but I know. He was thinking of Calvin, going back through the moments, big and little, trying to figure out where it went wrong.

I press my hand to his hip, silently telling him I'll listen if he wants to talk, but instead, in the next second, his face is buried in my shoulder.

For a second, I think I've made him cry again, but then he says, "I don't think I can watch this."

"The flyers? Why not?"

"I'm afraid of heights."

I laugh. "My poor, sweet teddy bear. Do you want me to tell you what's happening?"

He nods, but at no time does he lift his head.

So I do. I wrap my arm around his shoulders and hold him close. His hair is soft under my cheek as I describe the way they climb to the top, high in the sky, while one of them plays music. The crowd around us gasps as the men lean back and fall free, the pole turning as they slowly unwind from the ropes attached to their ankles, while streamers trail from the headpieces they wear.

When they're about halfway down, Doug turns his head, keeping it on my chest, but he watches as they finish the rest of their journey to the ground.

"Oh. That's so amazing." His voice is high and breathy, full of wonder. "Look at them. It's beautiful."

He's so open and honest, all his feelings on display, and now I get to be part of this with him too.

That's the moment I start to fall in love with Doug Freeman.

———

The bus takes us back to the ship. We're full of tequila and sunshine, and we half doze on the short trip to the port, both of us bumping against each other but quiet.

As we board again, they check us in, scanning our ship cards. When they scan mine, the woman pauses and frowns at the screen, then says, "Oh. Mr. Gillingham. Your luggage was delivered. It's in your cabin."

I'd completely forgotten about my bags. Wearing three-day-old underwear and tacky ship shirts doesn't seem so bad when you've got good company.

"Should we hang out by the pool?" Doug asks.

"That sounds like an amazing idea." With my clothes here now, I'll have the bathing suit I like better. I walk a lot of dogs and have killer legs. Why not show them off?

"Tripp?" Doug calls, and when I turn my head, pain I'd mostly forgotten pulls between my neck and shoulder.

"Ow." I wince, digging my thumb into the stiff spot. "Sorry. You were saying?"

"Nothing. I—I'll come grab you in a bit?"

He can grab me any time he wants.

"Yeah, sure."

Doug scratches his belly, like he's thinking about something. "Do you—" He clears his throat.

"What's the matter, snap pea?"

He rolls his eyes. "How many pet names do you have?"

How long will I have to keep coming up with them? Feeling mischievous—or maybe tipsy from the tequila—I say, "Honey, I can go all night."

He blushes and coughs. I think I hear him mutter, "Good to know," which makes me tighten inside.

The feeling gets worse when he asks, "Do you want to sleep in my room?"

Oh, sweet baby Jesus in a basket. "Excuse me?"

He rubs a hand over his neck. "I didn't sleep well last night. Haven't slept well since we got here, actually. But I felt better today. With you. It was easier not to dwell on the wedding and Calvin. So I was thinking—" His gaze drops. "Never mind."

"No." I feel a bit breathless, like I was one of those flyers tumbling slowly from the top of the pole until my head brushed the grass "Go on, ask."

He squares his shoulders. "The couch in my suite is a pull-out. You could sleep there. Maybe just for tonight. I'll ask guest services for an extra room key."

Holy fucking shit balls. Maybe I started to fall in love with him as we watched Mexican rain dancers gracefully float to the ground and he let me hold him, but this is the moment I realize it. Doug is a man I could be desperately in love with in very short order.

Which is why I should stay in my own room. Liam's gone. I'll have the bed and all the pillows to myself. And I'll be able to keep a buffer between Doug and my poor selfish feelings.

But I am a weak, weak man, so I say, "Yeah. Of course. Let me get my suitcase."

9

DOUG

ripp snores. Not a lot, but Calvin used to sleep like the dead. Just lie there and breathe so shallowly you hardly knew he was there. Tripp has an ongoing purr that starts from the minute he closes his eyes until the morning *bong bong* wakes us up.

Well, it wakes Tripp up. I wish I could say his presence in my room helped me sleep, but I've been awake for hours, after a series of increasingly weird dreams where Calvin and I are having dinner and Tripp joins us, and he and Calvin act like they're best friends, while I'm left trying to get Tripp's attention to ask him what he wants to eat, even though I know the answer is grasshoppers.

The hum of the ship makes it feel like a giant animal has swallowed us and is slowly carrying us across the ocean to its watery lair.

Today's activity is snorkeling.

My stomach cramps anxiously while Tripp purrs on the pull-out couch.

Calvin said I could plan the honeymoon any way I wanted, but when I told him the itinerary I was looking at stopped in the

Cayman Islands, he immediately said he wanted to go snorkeling.

"Some of the best snorkeling in the world," he said. "We'd be idiots to skip it."

I am not a strong swimmer. When I was a kid, my parents sent me to summer camp a few times, but it never really took. Too active. Too loud. The food was too unpredictable, and I never figured out how to not overheat in my sleeping bag. The mandatory swim hour in the afternoon was an overwhelming throng of splashing and shouting, and most days I wound up sitting on the beach.

But Calvin wanted to go snorkeling, and I wanted to make Calvin happy, because planning the wedding was making us both miserable.

Were we miserable before we got engaged? Of course, it was pretty much all misery after my dad died, but I assumed that had to do with him. If it turns out Calvin was contributing to my unhappiness, I don't know what I'll do with that information.

"Why would you want to lie on the beach all day? We can practically do that here. We'll never see reefs like this anywhere."

I'd been drawn to Calvin because he pushed me. Took me places I wouldn't go otherwise, made me try things I thought were too frightening. And he took care of me when everything else was awful.

"Come on. Let's just go for a walk. Doesn't have to be far. You'll feel better if you get out of the house."

But was that why I wanted to marry him? So he could keep challenging me? And what did it say about him that he thought I needed to be changed?

Tripp snorts as the morning announcements begin and rolls over, burying his head under his pillow. The sheet slides down, exposing the expanse of his tanned back and shoulders. With his arms the way they are, the muscles under his skin are bunched and taut, and I'm trying not to look, but it's so hard.

Calvin was seven years older than me, and while I always thought he was handsome, his body showed his forty years and all the time he'd spent in offices instead of being outside or at the gym.

I don't think Tripp is thirty yet, even with his three degrees, and he clearly takes care of himself. He's not overly built, but right now, as he shifts and the sheet slips towards the curve at the base of his spine, I can't drag my eyes away.

A knock sounds at the door, and I hop out of bed. Breakfast is delivered, and the man with the tray doesn't say anything about the way my supposed husband is sleeping on the pullout, with his perfect tanned back on view for anyone to see.

Oh God. What if he's naked? I didn't see him get into bed last night. I'd gone to brush my teeth, and when I'd come back out, he was already under the covers, stretching experimentally. And watching him as the sun came up was a fun fantasy, but suddenly I am confronted with the prospect of his nude body as he gets out of bed.

I've seen it before. Why would it bother me now?

"Baby. It's been weeks," Calvin's voice croons in my head. *"I know you're stressed. We're both stressed. Let's help each other out."*

The last time we tried to have sex was humiliating. He kept kissing me and touching me, and no matter what he did, I couldn't get hard. I told him I was tired, that the pressure of the wedding and trying to plan for the office to run without me while we were away was making it tough to focus on him. He'd said he'd understood, but what I'd really wanted was for him to hold me, and instead he'd rolled away and turned out the light.

Tripp has shown me more kindness so far as my imaginary husband than Calvin had shown in months. Every conversation about the wedding was an opportunity for him to criticize. *"Are you sure your suit will fit?" "That's not really the song you want for our first dance, is it?" "Please, pick anything but Caesar salad for the menu." "I am not serving chicken to my boss."*

It was almost like, as I pulled my life back together and he didn't need to take care of me so much, he found new ways to nitpick and look for parts of me that could be better.

Tripp hadn't even laughed when I couldn't watch the flying men yesterday. Calvin always said my fear of heights was irrational. He said for my fortieth birthday, he wanted to take me on the EdgeWalk at the CN Tower. I kept telling myself he had years to forget about that little self-improvement plan.

Why was I with someone who was always trying to make me a better version of myself? Why wasn't the me he had enough?

Tripp stirs, and his head emerges from under the pillow. I take the coward's way out and dart into the bathroom. I run the faucet until steam rises from the sink and soak a facecloth, pressing it over my cheeks. Tripp said strictly PG. I can't delude myself into thinking I am anything other than a pity case to him, no matter how I might imagine what his skin would feel like under my hands. When the cruise is over, we'll get a fake divorce and go our separate ways.

He's sitting up when I come out of the bathroom. The sheets are now pooled around his knees and waist. He's got a small plate of mini Danishes on the covers beside him, and he blows over a cup of coffee to cool it.

"Good morning." He gives me a sleepy smile that makes my breath catch.

Smiling is PG-13, isn't it?

"Sleep okay?" I try not to be weird as I serve myself some fruit and pastries and pour coffee of my own.

"Mm." He rolls his head on his shoulders, and his smile becomes satisfied, like a cat's, and the thoughts that fill my head are once again most definitely not family friendly. I don't want to be the weirdo perving on my fake husband, but Tripp is making it very hard—er—difficult. Very, very difficult.

"I'm going to eat on the balcony," I say, even though it still seems impossibly high above the water. Maybe if I keep the seat as close to the sliding door as possible, I'll be okay.

"Oh, I'll join you." Tripp flicks the sheet away, and my eyes widen, until I catch the glimpse of his waistband and the race-car-print boxer briefs he's wearing after all.

I don't know if I should be relieved or disappointed, especially when he makes no move to put any more clothes on as he follows me outside. We're relatively protected on the balcony. There's no way for anyone above or below to see us, and we're separated from our neighbors by full panels of frosted glass that make it hard to distinguish anything clearly. Somewhere to my left, a man calls to a woman about where she put the sunscreen, but I couldn't say if it's the people in the suite next to us or farther down.

Tripp settles into one of the patio chairs with his foot propped up against the balcony rail. The bulge in the front of his underwear is not insubstantial, and I can't help the memory that bubbles up from that first afternoon in the hallway. I know he's well equipped. At the time, I never thought—

I shove three pieces of honeydew into my mouth at once, nearly choking, but it's the distraction I need to not imagine Tripp's body against mine, his cock in my hand while—

Nope. Shit. I'm imagining it anyway.

"So, what's on the plan for today, captain?" Tripp says. Christ, my face must be the same colour as the watermelon on my plate, and he doesn't even seem to notice. *Exactly.* I tell myself. *He doesn't notice. He doesn't think of you like that.*

"Snorkeling." It's out so fast I forget that I'm not sure I even want to go.

Tripp says, "Oh, awesome!" with a big smile, and my fate is sealed.

Like yesterday, we gather at a signpost. We're about twenty people again, although no one I recognize from the tequila group. I take a quick survey of my fellow snorkelers. A few teenagers traveling with their parents. Lots of thirty- and forty-somethings. One couple who must be in their eighties. He's got a cane, and she's hunched over in a way that makes me ache just looking at her.

If they can do this, surely I can too?

Tripp talks up a storm on the little minibus that picks us up, making friends fast and easy. He's clearly put some thought into our backstory since yesterday. We live in Toronto. We met at a film shoot where I had come to interview someone about being a queer mainstream actor, and he was there helping the dog trainers wrangle a frisky pack of four-legged actors. One of the dogs got loose, and I helped him catch it.

Never mind that I never leave my office or that celebrity dog trainer is a far cry from doggie day care. People buy into every thing he says, and the longer he talks, the more I relax into their friendly banter and the hand that always seems to be touching me, whether on my back, around one shoulder, or wrapped around my hand.

Calvin's friends always made me nervous. They all worked in finance like he did, and their conversations always seemed to be about one-upmanship. Who had the new promotion, the new assistant? Where were they taking their next vacation? What trendy new thing were they into—juicing, meditation, or goat yoga? If you didn't have the right answer, their gaze would trail off somewhere over your right shoulder, like you weren't impor-tant enough to pay attention to.

Tripp seems genuinely excited by everything people say to him, whether it's that they're on their first cruise or that they're a high school principal from Missouri.

"How do you do that?" I ask as we're helped onto the boat.

"Do what?" His hand is firm in mine as we step on board. After days on the floating monolith known as the *Tropical Vista*, getting onto something that actually bobs under your feet is disorienting.

"You seem so glad to meet everyone."

He laughs. "I learned. When I was in grad school . . . it was so cliquey. I was eighteen months into my PhD and suddenly everything got so secretive. Your research, your funding." Tripp rolls his eyes. "Especially the funding. I kept studying because I loved my subject, but I looked at the track ahead of me, at the cutthroat way people fought for money and jobs, and I knew I didn't want to do that. When I stepped away, I took a long, hard look at my biases."

"Biases?"

Our conversation takes a pause as we're given a formal welcome aboard and then a brief safety orientation while the boat pulls away from the dock.

Tripp has his face turned up to the sun, eyes closed, as we motor out into the open ocean. He's so calm, so relaxed, when I'm doing my best not to think about what's coming, that I hate to disturb him, but I'm also curious about what he meant.

"You were saying?"

"Hm?" He glances at me with one eye open. "Oh. Biases." He rubs his cheek against his bare shoulder, and for a second, he looks nervous. "I guess it's safe to say I come from money, even though people always get weird about it when I tell them. My dad was a developer and bought a lot of real estate in Vancouver through the eighties and nineties. It's paid him back handsomely. And he used that money to build a nice life for him, my mom—both while they were married and then in spousal support—his second wife, and me too. I thought that was what it meant to be happy. Get an education, get a job, know the right people. But school wasn't making me happy, and I knew I didn't want a job like my dad's. When I told him I wanted to start my own business, he thought I'd get into something more glamorous than looking after other people's dogs. He was so worried I'd shame his good name somehow. 'What will people say?' That's literally what he asked me. Can you believe that shit?"

"What does that have to do with biases, though?" I ask.

He shrugs. "He thought what I wanted to do wasn't good enough. But you never know. People who don't do white collar jobs aren't less interesting. Sometimes they're actors who wait tables. Or they're mechanics who build their own remote-control airplanes from scratch. Everybody is so interesting. It doesn't matter what it says on their business card, or if they even have one."

It's the most he's said about himself since we met. He's been so focused on me that I didn't know any of this. But even while he's saying the nicest things about people, his shoulders are slowly creeping up towards his ears with tension. Whatever peace he's come to about his decision now, Tripp's still holding some old family grief under it. I wonder if I'll have the same reaction about Calvin in a few years. "Oh yeah, I was engaged once before. Funny story about that . . . " At least I don't feel like crying or throwing up at the very thought of his name this morning. But I wouldn't go so far as to say I can laugh.

What I can do, though, is let Tripp know I get it. Or that I don't care what he does for a living as long as it's honest and meaningful. Without our sponsors, Out & About would still be a bunch of queer film geeks getting together on Friday nights to scour the internet for any new movie listings where the gay character isn't an accessory or cautionary tale.

As my hand moves, I realize I've never touched him before. I mean, we've touched, but he's always been the one to initiate it. He's looking out over the water, so I put a hand on his shoulder and then let it slide to the back of his neck, running my fingers through the prickly edges of his hair where it's cut short. He shivers before he leans into it. I hesitate, but when I press gently on the muscle there, Tripp closes his eyes and moans.

Now we're both shivering, even though the sun is bright and it won't be this hot in Toronto for six months or more.

I shuffle closer on the bench seat we've claimed, and he

sighs, dropping his head to my shoulder. No one seems to notice or care about the two gay guys cuddling, so I press my cheek to his hair and watch the turquoise ocean zip by.

"Who's your favourite dog, apart from Trixie?"

He laughs softly but doesn't move. "I'm not supposed to have favourites."

"Come on." I nudge him. "They're not your children. And some people's dogs are spoiled, yappy assholes. You have to have a favourite."

Tripp rolls his head, so his cheek is pressed more to my chest than my shoulder, and says, "There's this one dog. Morton. He's got three legs and the best smile you've ever seen."

———

We arrive at our destination after about a half hour. Tripp and I have had a long and detailed conversation about each of the dogs he looks after regularly. I know about Morton and about Louie—the Chorkie who doesn't care that he only weighs seven pounds while he's defending his favourite sunny spot from dogs ten times his size. Whatever baggage Tripp is carrying about his family, it's obvious he loves what he does, the people he works with, and the parts of the city he gets to see every day while taking his doggie clients out on adventures.

I'm so enthralled by the story of Bella the Staffordshire bull terrier who comes to daycare every day in a tutu that I don't even notice we've arrived until Tripp's story is interrupted by the clatter of the anchor as it drops over the side of the boat. Tripp pops up excitedly and peels off his shirt. He's switched from the printed swim trunks he wore the day by the pool to a navy and green speedo that swirls color around his ass and shows off the strong tone of his thighs. His stomach is flat and lightly hairy. I should be mesmerized, like I was while he was in bed, but instead the anxious feeling in my stomach returns in a rush.

"Are you okay?" Tripp asks.

I blink, fighting back the nervousness. The elderly couple is pulling snorkel masks from a backpack, which means they've brought their own gear. Where before they were sweet and comforting, now I'm intimidated.

"Fine."

But as the ship's crew hands out masks and fins to those of us who haven't brought our own, my hands shake.

"You sure?" Tripp asks.

I give him my bravest smile. It's the one I gave Calvin when he suggested something I didn't want to do and I knew he wouldn't accept my refusal. "Yes."

"Pepper blossom." His voice drops in a warning, and I laugh when I realize I'm the pepper blossom. His pet names are so ridiculous.

I sigh. "I'm not a very good swimmer." I brace for him to ask why we're even here if I don't like swimming.

Instead, one of the crew members overhears me and says, "We have life vests, if you'd be more comfortable." She holds out a yellow inflatable vest, like the kind they tell you about in airplane safety demos but you never actually use. I take an involuntary step back, because accepting the vest somehow feels even more embarrassing than admitting I'm not super comfortable with what we're about to do.

Tripp laces his hand with mine. "Butternut, we don't have to do this if you don't want to. We can stay on the boat and enjoy the sun."

Staying is really tempting. If he were Calvin and had offered this, I'd jump on it immediately. But I want Tripp to like me so badly. And somehow, I'm annoyed he's being nice.

As though to remind him of a discussion we already had, even though it wasn't Tripp who was there, I say, "But it's the Caymans. Best snorkeling in the world."

"It's not far," the woman with the life vest says. "The wreck is about a hundred feet that way." She points to an open expanse of water that looks utterly similar to all the other water around it: blue and very deep. Don't get me wrong. I *can* swim. I'm just moderately terrified of being in open water where I can't get to the bottom and have nothing solid to hold on to.

"We don't have to," Tripp says again.

I take the vest and pull it on.

Tripp watches me with a frown, but I ignore him and climb down the ladder, fumbling to put my flippers on the way I've been instructed.

He's sitting on the edge of the boat, feet dangling in the water. His lips are pursed, and he hasn't put his mask on.

"Come on!" I say, surprised at the anger bubbling just beneath my skin and trying to hide my embarrassment. I don't want him to treat me like a child. "I signed us up for this damn excursion, and we're going to do it."

The spark of laughter is back in his eye. "And the bloom is off the marital rose already. What's that? Four days. Good job, squeegee."

Before I can ask when the hell that became a term of endearment, Tripp pushes off and plunges in. I turn my head to dodge the splash, and when I look back, he's bobbed up and is shaking the water out of his hair before he takes his mask, snorkel, and fins from the boat staff.

The first time I put my face in the ocean, a line of silvery fish with needle-like noses is so close that I spit out my snorkel and suck in a mouthful of salt water. I bob back up, coughing and spluttering. Tripp is right by my shoulder, but it's the woman on the boat who asks if I'm okay.

This is the moment I should say I've changed my mind. I'm on my goddamned honeymoon, after all; I can do what I like. Who cares if I spend the day sipping rum punches and working on my tan?

Instead, I wave her and Tripp off, put the snorkel back in,

and plunge my face into the water again. The fish are gone and, after a second, I find it's not that hard to breathe as long as I don't panic. Without further hesitation, I kick my feet and make my way towards where the other tourists are floating facedown.

Snorkeling is more work than I expected, not like swimming in a pool. The wind is up and the water is a bit wavy, so I have to kick pretty hard, even with the fins. But the life vest keeps me from worrying about sinking, and within a minute or two, I'm less concerned about the snorkel filling with water and drowning me, because my brain finally wraps around the fact I can lift my head any time I want and be able to breath sweet, sweet air.

And then we come to the wreck.

It's an old submarine. Farther down than the shadow looked from the boat, but the depth only leaves more room for the magic. Fingers of green, orange, and purple coral reach up towards me, and bright fish in every colour dart in and out of the coral and the dark shadows of the submarine like something straight from a Disney movie.

I swim up the length of it, transfixed. It's just . . . there. Silent and permanent, while everything else around it is alive. A wave splashes over my head, dribbling water into my snorkel, and I don't even care, blowing hard to spit it back out again, because a school of electric yellow and silver fish are swimming just below me. If I reach out a hand, I feel like I could touch them.

My shoulder bumps against something, and when I pop up, Tripp is there.

"You okay?" he asks, his voice sounding weird because of the way his nose is trapped in the mask.

"Did you see the fish?"

He laughs. "There are a lot of fish."

"No. The yellow ones. They—" I put my face back in the water, paddling myself around in a tight circle before coming back up again. "They were right here. It was amazing."

Tripp smiles. "So you're okay? Don't want to go back to the boat?"

"Are you kidding? We're almost at the end of the submarine. Then I'm going to do it all over again!"

I kick off again, working hard. I have a theory, and I'm delighted to find I'm right once I'm out over sandy ocean floor.

I've been swimming against the waves and wind this whole time. When I turn around, I don't have to swim at all. The water carries me back down the full length of the submarine. I hardly even need to steer. My one task is to take in all the beauty around me, and it is incredible. The fish weave below me and the coral waves in gentle undulations completely at odds with the busy wind at my back.

A hand grazes my wrist, and I turn to find Tripp there. I go to give him a thumbs-up, to reassure him that I really am okay, but he's pointing excitedly a ways off from the submarine. I swim in the direction he's indicating, sticking close to Tripp's shoulder. I can't figure out what he wants me to see, but then he's pointing down and just in front of us excitedly, and I spot it.

The sea turtle is mottled with deep green and electric lime. From up here, it looks like it has to be at least three feet across the top of its shell. Its curved fins paddle lazily up and down, as if the cumbersome body behind them doesn't weigh a thing.

I find Tripp's hand and squeeze. He squeezes back, and we follow the turtle for a while. It doesn't seem to mind having us as spectators any more than it minds the swirling schools of fish as it makes its way along the far side of the reef before heading out into deeper water. We slow, watching it go, before we drift back and follow the path of the submarine again. Tripp holds my hand the whole time.

10

TRIPP

I think we know each other well enough by now that you can tell I haven't been a monk. My Serial Monogamy Disorder is real. I've never been single for more than a few weeks at a time since I was in high school, which is to say I've had plenty of opportunities to test out other partners and develop a strong sense of what does and does not do it for me.

The first one is guys who are good with their hands. No, not like that, get your mind out of the gutter. A guy who knows how to fix things—*really* fix things, not just take your blender apart, curse, and bang around for a while before pitching the whole thing and buying a new one—is frigging hot. I'm pretty much only capable of emptying the lint trap in the dryer and changing the vacuum bag. A guy who can actually figure out why my dishwasher won't stop beeping is a dream come true. I have yet to seduce the man who comes to my house to rewire my bedroom lighting, but that doesn't mean I haven't thought about it.

The next turn-on is guys who love their dogs. Not a *this is Fifi, a vicious bitch who will tear your face off, but I love her anyway* kind of love. People who can't be bothered to train their dogs don't deserve the privilege of dog ownership. But I have one client, Max, whose dog—oddly also called Max—has wicked separa-

85

tion anxiety. And human Max goes above and beyond to make sure that dog Max doesn't get too stressed out while he's with me. We've got human-Max-scented blankets and FaceTime recordings to play when dog Max starts to worry. Some people may think this is spoiling your pet, but I think it's beautiful. Tragically, Max is very straight—human Max, that is; dog Max has never expressed a preference in romantic partners, although he does get moony-eyed when Sparkles the Australian shepherd is at daycare—and happily married.

The third thing—a very new addition—is trivia nerds. Guys who can rattle off random facts about pop culture, international politics, and astronomy. Yeah, turns out Tripp Chet-Bryson Free-man-Gillingham is kind of a slut for that specific type of nerdiness.

Fortunately, his new pretend husband is exactly that sort of geek.

This new kink of mine is discovered after dinner. Dougie has a reservation for us at the Mediterranean restaurant on board. He orders chicken on Israeli couscous but picks all the raisins out. I order broiled fish with an artichoke puree. I also eat all of Doug's rejected raisins.

As we're finishing dinner, I ask, "So what do you want to do tonight?"

He glances at me quickly, like I've surprised him with my very mundane question. He's been quiet since we got back from snorkeling; I'm not sure why. He did so great out there. I wouldn't have cared if he backed out, but the whole experience —from the amazing wreck to the way we followed that sea turtle —was pretty incredible.

"Do you want to call it a night?" I ask, exaggerating my stretch. I'm not tired. It was a busy day, and we ate late here on the ship, but if he says he wants to keep the party going, I'm all for that.

I'll be for that for as long as he wants me.

Too bad I only negotiated for a week.

He runs a finger through the caramel drizzle smeared on the plate in front of him, then sucks it into his mouth. I glance away, because thinking about flipping away the table between us so I can suck on his finger too is not a constructive use of my time.

While Doug was showering after we got back, I went down to the business center to check my email. There was one reply from Pierce, in response to the one I'd sent two days ago.

I told you so. DO NOT fall in love with anyone on that ship. It will only end in tears.

P

He knows me so well.

But he's right. When I fall, I fall hard. Liam and I had been on three dates when the lease ran out on my previous apartment and I suggested we move in together. In the last six years, I have lived in eleven different apartments and condos in Vancouver. Pierce tells me that kind of lifestyle isn't sustainable, and it's true that I know exactly how many boxes I need to pack up all my stuff right down to the cubic inch, which probably isn't something most people know.

"There's trivia at the aft bar," Doug says before he does another pass with his finger over the plate. Goddammit, he needs to stop doing that.

Trivia. Time to focus on trivia.

"Oh yeah? Is that a thing you do?"

He smiles softly, index finger between his lips. "Yeah. I'm not bad."

Not bad, my ass. As I find out very quickly, my little woodchuck is a freaking genius.

The bar is pretty quiet when we walk in. A few people sitting in little round banquettes towards the back. A few more milling about. But when a woman in a *Tropical Vista* uniform walks onto the small stage at one side of the room and announces trivia will be starting in five minutes, it's like each person around me spontaneously reproduces and stampedes—along with their two clones—to collect the official trivia answer page and branded golf pencil from the stage.

Doug doesn't say anything as he grabs his supplies and finds a seat. I sort of follow him around, not sure what I should do. I've seen trivia nights advertised in bars but never actually been to one.

"Um, are we supposed to pair up? Make teams?"

Doug grins up at me. "Team Gillingham-Freeman!"

I snort. "That's Freeman-Gillingham."

But he shuffles over on the bench seat to give me space, and I squeeze in next to him, letting myself press along his body from our shoulders to our knees.

"I should warn you, I'm probably going to drag you down."

His smile is wicked when he pats my thigh and says, "I didn't marry you for your trivia skills, babe."

It takes a second for me to realize Doug is *excited*. Like really pumped. He spreads the answer sheet on the table in front of him and arranges his stubby little pencils at the top in a neat row. His fingers drum a steady rhythm as he looks at the people sitting near us.

"Sizing up the competition?" I ask playfully, but he doesn't respond as his eyes roam around the room.

Oh.

Something quivers in my chest before it goes hot and spreads in my limbs. Doug's features, on which I have seen every emotion from sadness and disappointment to quiet joy and awe, are hard now. Almost stern.

This is his game face.

I'm weirdly turned on by it. Suddenly I can imagine what Doug's like as an alpha male. He's had a hard day at the office. Maybe he won a case, and he stalks through the house as he commands me—in a voice that gets me instantly hard—to take my clothes off and go to the bedroom.

Except Doug's anything but an alpha male, and instead of being full of that "fuck yeah" confidence after a big lawyerly win or going toe-to-toe in a boxing ring, he's slowly puffing himself up in anticipation of a cruise ship trivia night.

My pretend husband is fucking adorable.

The woman acting as our host reappears and spells out the rules. Teams of two to four. No phones for help—not that we have signal out here anyway—and ten questions in each category. The team with the highest point total at the end of four rounds is the winner.

I'm suddenly nervous, even though the prize is no doubt a pack of logoed playing cards or fifty bucks in on-board credit. But Doug is tapping his pencil on the edge of the table, and I can feel his leg bobbing against mine.

Game on.

The first round is all about famous politicians. She's got a screen that shows pictures of white dudes in suits, and we're supposed to name them. I sort of recognize a few. Others are complete strangers. Sometimes, I say something like, "Well, it could be—" before realizing Doug is already writing down his answer.

His intensity is cute the first few times. By question six, though, I'm a little annoyed. We're a team here, and he's not even giving me a chance to answer. And what does he know about food?

Except when he hands in his answers and the hostess counts them up, he's gotten us a perfect score.

I lean back and order us a couple drinks, very aware of my place here.

"How did you know all that?"

He shrugs. "I read a lot. Watch a lot of documentaries. The last woman, Jóhanna Sigurðardóttir, was the first outwardly queer elected head of state."

I do my best not to distract him in round two. It's science and technology, which I'm basically useless in, except I know the question about when the first iPhone was released. Doug only gets eight points instead of the ten, and I can tell he's beating himself up for not remembering the difference between Galileo and Copernicus, even though I can't even spell Copernicus.

Two tables over, a team who must be father-daughter—if their white-blond hair and icy blue eyes are anything to go by—gets nine points. There's lots of high-fiving when the scores are announced. Doug tenses, and I catch him side-eyeing them. I want to giggle at this nerdy competitive streak he's showing me. I want to rub his shoulders and tell him we'll get them next time.

I want to get down on my knees and suck him off until he's screaming my name.

The next round goes better. The topic is classic movies. Doug shoots the father-daughter team a glance as his lips press into a confident smile. The expression has me wishing I had a pillow or a towel I could put over my lap to hide the half chub I'm currently sporting as it threatens to turn into something more urgent and noticeable. With every scratch of Doug's pencil on his paper, my blood pressure goes up.

This must be who he is when he's not confused and heart-broken. Calvin really did a number on him, but now I can see the man a banking executive might be attracted to. He's focused, determined, and the space between his eyebrows puckers as he pauses halfway through an answer, erases it, and writes something new. Even his jaw is tighter, clenched under the fuzz of his beard as he waits impatiently for the next question.

Maybe I can convince him to abandon his race for trivia dominance and take me back to our suite where he can dominate me instead.

Doug gets nine out of ten on the film round. He curses as she reads out the answers.

"I knew I shouldn't have changed that one."

"Always go with your gut," I murmur. My gut is saying if I

don't find a way to get Doug to fuck me before we land in Florida, I will regret it forever and ever.

Except I promised him to be hands-off. Promised not to mess with his damaged heart. And I may fall hard more often than Toronto Maple Leafs fans delude themselves into thinking this year is the year, but I know the way sex can screw with your emotions, and I can't do that to Doug.

The father-daughter team gets a perfect ten. Their smug grins in our direction make Doug's knuckles go white around his golf pencil.

I put a hand on his shoulder. "You'll get them in this last round. Only two points behind. You can totally do it, my little kitten whisker."

He doesn't react to the pet name at all. Every atom of his attention is on the woman at the front who doesn't know these final questions will make or break my sex life.

She holds up a set of cue cards. "The last category is . . . nicknames!"

Holy fuck, it's hard. Did you know Peggy is a nickname for Margaret? What sense does that even make? I sure as hell didn't know. But Doug does. The woman hasn't even finished speaking and he's got it written down.

And oh my God. Nancy? Is another name for Ann? How is that possible? It's got two more letters. Doug writes his answer with such authority the lead on his pencil snaps. Good thing he has two more. I half fight the urge to look around us, flag someone down, and ask for a towel and some ice chips so I can keep my husband cool while he fights through this championship round.

I throw a look at our competition. The daughter is watching us, and when her eyes meet mine, they narrow. I arch an eyebrow and tell myself that giving her a little wave would be petty. Still, her lips tighten, and her head goes back to her paper, whispering hurriedly to her partner.

"You've got this," I say softly to Doug, smoothing my hand over his back.

And then.

Oh my ever-loving Lord Stanley of the ice rink.

Then.

The woman reading the questions holds up her tenth card and reads, "What five-letter nickname is used to denote the third man in a sequence to share a name, usually with his father and grandfather?"

Doug's pencil pauses on the paper.

The space between my ears goes white with static.

He starts to write the first letter, but I know whatever he thinks the answer is, he's wrong, because the pencil isn't in the right spot.

My breathing is coming fast.

He lifts the pencil back up, puts it back down, draws a quarter inch of something that might be an A.

I put my shaking hand on top of his to stop him.

Doug's head whips up, so close our noses brush. "What?"

I'm smiling so hard my cheeks hurt. "That's not the answer."

He frowns and nods, eyes dropping down to the page, like he already knew that but couldn't think of anything else.

I lick my lips as I lean in. His hair brushes against my forehead, while my nose grazes his temple.

Doug freezes next to me.

Finding the air I need seems to take forever, but when the words finally coalesce and spill out from my mouth to his ear, I can barely contain my excitement. "Tripp." The hand under mine twitches, so I say again, more firmly. "The answer is Tripp."

He half turns towards me, so my mouth isn't in line with his ear anymore, but the corner of his lips instead. They're soft and pink, and the tip of his tongue peeks out to wet them, making me moan against his skin.

Doug writes my name in precise block letters on the sheet,

and then spreads his hand over it, as if he's worried someone will copy it like seventh-grade math homework.

I want to clap as he turns his answers in, and his cheeks are flushed as he comes back to our table. We hold our breath, hands wrapped around each other's, as the hostess reads out the questions and the correct answers. When she gets to the last one, she says my name. Doug hisses, while the father-daughter duo groan softly.

We win a pack of playing cards. And a mug.

I pull Doug out onto the open deck outside the bar. He smiles at me sheepishly while I dance, giddy, under the stars.

"Holy shit. You're like a trivia superhero!" I say.

"I just know random things."

"That's not random. That's work. How do you know all that?"

He shrugs. "I just do."

I put my hands on his shoulders, making sure he knows how serious I am. "You were incredible. Like so fierce. It was amazing to watch you do it. Orgasmic, even. I was so turned on I—"

Doug kisses me.

I didn't mean to say orgasmic. Or that I have a trivia fetish I am only just discovering. I promised myself I would do whatever it took to keep Doug from being sad, and I wanted him to know how impressive he'd been.

But I also promised him and myself that our arrangement wouldn't be sexual. Now his lips are on mine, and before I can even inhale, his tongue is pressing into my mouth. My hands are stuck, because they're holding the little paper gift bags with the mug and the playing cards in them, so I can't do anything but comply as he pushes into me, walking us backwards until my ass hits the rail, and I grunt.

"Doug."

He either doesn't hear or doesn't care. His hands are on my face, holding me where he wants, tilting my chin up to get the angle he needs, and the confidence in his grip makes me whimper pathetically. Yes, I've spent the last hour in a state of weird trivia-induced arousal, but I should not be this turned on from a single kiss.

Except it's Doug. Doug who isn't afraid to cry in front of me. Who invited me to share his room and doesn't roll his eyes at my pet names and half-baked plans like pretending to be my husband. His body on mine is hungry and strong and I know—*I know*—we're going to be great together.

"Doug. Please Doug." I've never thought of Doug as being a particularly romantic name. It's like looking into your partner's eyes and saying, "Oh, Ralph, do me right now." But with this Doug—*my* Doug—I don't care what his name is, as long as he'll keep kissing me. I know we said we weren't going to do this, and if there's anything I need, it's to not fall for the next guy who kisses me, but maybe I should make an exception, one last time.

"Yeah. Yeah." I gasp for words and air in the brief spaces where his mouth leaves mine, while his hands start to move over my body. Those hands gripped that stupid little pencil with all the intensity and determination of a fencer at a match. He's going to touch me like that until I'm begging, I just know it.

"Yes. Yes. Calv—"

The word gets cut off before it gets all the way out, and frankly, I don't even care that it's not mine.

But Doug cares. I can feel how he stiffens in an instant. One second he's about to consume me with his giant brain and those firm lips and hot hands of his, and the next he goes still.

No. No, no. Maybe I say that out loud. I reach for him, even though I'm still holding the stupid gift bags.

Doug is backing away, blinking quickly, like he's just waking up from a dream.

Please, please don't let him wake up.

"I—" His voice is rough.

"Babe?" The word wobbles in my throat. "It's okay. It's okay, I don't—"

But he shakes his head, taking another step, opening up more space between us until I want to cry.

"I—" He runs a hand over his mouth, wiping our kiss away. "I need to go for a walk."

"Doug?"

But he turns his back to me and hurries away.

11

DOUG

I called him Calvin. Never mind that I stopped halfway. He knows, I know. And in calling him Calvin, I realized I hadn't actually thought about Calvin in—what—hours? Had I thought about him at all today?

For a moment there, as Tripp whispered his name in my ear like it was the magic word to release the universe's secrets, I felt like myself again. More, in fact, like myself than I can remember feeling in a very long time.

When did I lose me? Was it as we planned the wedding? Before Calvin proposed? Why did I let go of myself?

A cruise ship, if you walk from one end to the other, is about a thousand feet long. You can literally walk miles if you cover every single level, and I do.

When my miles are done, I head back to our floor, which is dark as I make my way down the hall. I stumble as I nearly walk past the Day-Glo leprechaun, then I stand outside the suite door for what feels like hours. I can't make myself go in. If he's in there, I don't think I can face him, and if he's gone back to his own suite, I'll just feel lonelier than I already do. I never kissed Calvin the way I kissed Tripp tonight, and that knowledge makes me feel incredibly guilty.

But also, why did Calvin never kiss me like that? I mean, yeah, there's not much room for romance when your whole life is "we're sorry, your father isn't responding to treatment." But never? Why did I decide that was the kind of relationship I wanted?

I rest my head on the door, desperate for someone to tell me what to do. Then I nearly face-plant as the door swings open from inside. Tripp. Of course he's been waiting for me. And of course he catches me before I hurt myself.

"Sorry. Sorry," I say as he says, "Are you okay?"

We stare at each other for a long time. The room is dark, but I can make out the white shapes of our opposing beds. The idea of crawling into mine feels so lonely.

"I have to pee." I don't, but it gives me the space I need. I duck into the small washroom and sit on the closed toilet lid, hands in my face. What am I supposed to do? If I go back out there, maybe Tripp will tell me not to freak out, that one kiss is just what fake husbands do, and I shouldn't read more into it than that.

But the soft noises he made as he kissed me did not sound fake. I want him, more than I've wanted Calvin in longer than I can remember.

I'm suddenly angry. Not at myself or at Tripp, but at Calvin. Here I am, agonizing over kissing someone, when Calvin had the audacity to just not show up for our wedding. Those few seconds after I called Tripp by the wrong name, I felt so much guilt, and Calvin couldn't even be bothered to tell me he didn't want to get married to my face.

I'm tired of reacting. Tired of bobbing around in this ocean instead of doing things for myself. I've let it go on for too long.

Which is great to tell myself in the confined space of the bathroom. It's another when faced with the person I most want on the receiving end of any action I might take.

Tripp's in his bed, his back to me, when I come out of the

bathroom, and my feet get stuck halfway across the room. The more I try to the move, the wobblier my whole body gets, until finally I stumble onto the edge of the pull-out mattress and slump down with a sigh. I can't do this. I was never the decisive one. I wanted to take charge, but instead all I manage to do is turn into a very sad blob, sitting in the dark.

The sheets rustle and the mattress shakes.

"Do you want to talk about it?" Based on the sound and direction of his voice, I can tell Tripp sat up, but he doesn't make any move to get closer.

"About accidentally calling you my fiancé's name?"

"Or about your mad trivia prowess. Or the way you kiss like you want to be someone's daddy, when the rest of you screams soft fuzzy teddy bear."

I shudder. "I'm so sorry."

"I'm not." He laughs softly. "But I won't expect you to do it again if you don't want to."

I shake my head. The tumble of thoughts going in circles inside it is making me dizzy. "I don't know what I want."

He slides forwards, the covers bunching up around his knees where he's braced his elbows. When he's next to me, he rests his chin on my shoulder. "It's not a big deal. I never expected anything physical from you. If you're not comfortable, we don't have to do it again. I'll even go back to my room if you want. But I'm really enjoying spending time with you."

"I am too." I keep staring ahead, because I've already learned tonight that if I turn to look at him, our lips will be so close it will be virtually impossible not to kiss him.

"But..."

I pick at my fingernails. "But Calvin..."

His chin is gone, leaving a draft on my neck. "Do you want to tell me about him?"

My heart—well, I don't actually know what my heart does when he asks that, but it's not fun.

What do you tell your fake husband—who maybe, in another life, could have been your real boyfriend—about your real fiancé who has been your boyfriend and partner for three years, but who, apparently, doesn't want the job anymore? And who, with every passing day, you're increasingly unsure ever really made you happy?

I start at the beginning. Well, not the *beginning*, but the point where our path from casual to committed really cemented itself. "My dad was diagnosed with pancreatic cancer about four months after Calvin and I started dating."

The silence fills with ship's engine static before Tripp asks, "Is your dad okay?"

He's so lucky that he doesn't automatically know the five-year survival rate for pancreatic cancer is only eight percent.

I shake my head. It's been two years, and I can talk about him now without turning into a rubbery sobbing mess, but it's still hard. "He made it about seven more months. And the whole time he was sick, Calvin was a rock. He'd come to the hospital with me. We'd go to my mom's and cook for her and do the shopping. He never complained when my sisters needed someone to babysit their kids."

"The perfect boyfriend," Tripp says softly.

He really had been. "And then, after my dad died, I was a mess for, like, a year. My dad was my hero and my best friend, and he was only sixty-one when he passed away. That's way too young."

Tripp's voice is rough when he says, "Yeah."

"For a while, I was only going to work a few days a week, because that was all I could manage. I stopped seeing my friends. Basically didn't leave the condo. And the whole time, Calvin was there with me. Sometimes he'd push, but I needed that, you know? Otherwise I would have been a total hermit." I tried, but after three or four days wearing the same underwear and living on pasta and jarred tomato sauce, Calvin would beg me to take a shower, and we'd go for a walk on the beach or get an ice cream and ride the streetcar, just to say I'd gotten some fresh air. "And then last Christmas, there was a tiny box under the tree at my mom's house, and he proposed, right there, in front of my whole family. He said I was the most important person in his life and he didn't want to be with anyone else and—"

I was so happy that morning in my parents' house, which was home to many family movie nights and Christmas mornings when I was growing up. And yes, I'd been aware of my family—my mom, my sisters, their husbands, their kids—sitting around me, and the excited tension that filled the room in the moments before I'd said yes. But saying no had never crossed my mind. In all the hazy sadness and grief that had come, starting the day my dad was diagnosed, Calvin had been there. How could I say no after all that?

But somewhere along the way, once I was able to look after myself again, his actions went from being about taking care of me to changing behaviour he found unpleasant or unacceptable.

I've stopped speaking. Mostly forgotten Tripp's even there, so I jump a bit when he says, "Are you still in love with him?"

I don't know anymore. Now I'm starting to doubt if I was ever in love with him. "The thing with my dad, it made it all so much more than big feelings, wearing each other's clothes, and giving each other cute names." I wince, because I love Tripp's pet names, but what Calvin and I had got so serious so fast.

"Are you—" Tripp's still somewhere behind me, but his voice is getting farther away, like he's trying to escape me. "When you get back to Toronto, will you try to work things out with him?"

I don't even know why he called off the wedding, so how do I know if there's anything to work out? Even if we were in love once, maybe he doesn't love me anymore. Or maybe my insisting on serving Caesar salad at the rehearsal dinner—since he didn't want it at the reception—was the final straw and he knows I'll never live up to his expectations.

And if that's the case, I don't think he's someone I want to be with.

"I don't know?" I feel like shit. This thing with Tripp, it was supposed to be fun, but somewhere along the way, I crossed a line, because now I feel guilty as hell that I dragged him into this mess. "Will you try to work things out with Liam when you go home?"

He snorts. "No. We're done. I'm not really boyfriend material. More like the goofy hipster with the novelty career who gives a great blow job."

"You're way more than that," I say, although the mention of the blow job makes my skin heat. In those few frenzied seconds when our mouths had met and I'd forgotten to think about anything but Tripp and how much I wanted him, I'd have done anything he asked.

"I'm sorry. I'm making a mess of things," I say.

"You're not." He touches me. Finally. Oh God, finally. I didn't know much I needed that small comfort until his hand is on my shoulder and he's pulling me gently, so we're both leaning against the back of the sofa and his arm is around me. How many times has he comforted me in the last few days?

"You're the best pretend husband a guy could ask for," I say. I'm suddenly tired in a way I haven't been since those months after my dad died, when all of my feelings were completely exhausting.

He scoots us down, and I feel the soft pressure of a blanket thrown over my thighs. I'm still in my clothes, but my tongue is too thick to protest, my eyelids too heavy to stay open. I must fight sleep for a minute, though, because I feel a soft kiss on my forehead, and Tripp whispers, "Shh. It's okay. Stay here with me."

Yes. I want that. Him. Here. He hasn't asked me for anything, other than to just be here with him. Calvin asked me for every-thing, tried to change anything he didn't like, and I let him, because it was easier when he made the decisions.

That ends now. Even if I fly back to Toronto and Calvin flings himself at my feet and begs me to forgive him, we won't be like we were before. If he only wants to be with the person he thinks I can become, then we aren't going to work anymore. I want to be with someone who thinks my extensive mental library of trivia facts is something to be proud of. I want to write down my own answers and make my own decisions, even if it's to order Caesar salad and chicken for dinner every single night.

I'll deal with what's coming later exactly then: later. Right now, I'm choosing to stay with Tripp.

12

TRIPP

I haven't slept with someone without . . . you know . . . *sleeping* with them first in probably close to ten years. Not since I came across from Vancouver Island—which, okay, when I say it like that, it sounds like a trek, but really it takes about ninety minutes—and then came out with a bang.

But sleeping with Doug is more intimate than any hookup or one-night stand.

At six in the morning, I untangle myself from his warm body and make my way down to the business center. I send an email to Pierce.

I'm so screwed.

T

Doug's still asleep as I let myself back into the suite. Still in his clothes from last night.

I'm starting to have regrets.

They are:

I couldn't possibly have known about his dad, but I'm sorry I didn't find out sooner.

I should never have proposed the fake husbands thing. Doug needs a real husband with a strong shoulder to lean on.

I regret that I've wasted so many days playing house when I

could have been really getting to know Doug, because I think we could be something special.

When I crawl back into bed, he rolls towards me, like he's been waiting. He slings an arm over my torso and sighs in his sleep. I run my fingers over the soft hairs on the back of his arm.

In order to be the boyfriend he needs, I'm going to have to give him up, even though he was never mine to begin with. He has to go back to Toronto. He needs to sort out whatever happened with Calvin—maybe even still marry him—and no amount of make-believe on a cruise ship will change that.

I bury my nose in his hair. We should talk about some of this, but for now, we'll sleep.

Except the next thing I know, the PA system is *bong bong*ing and Doug's telling the suite attendant to put our breakfast on the coffee table, and when I finally wake up enough to open my eyes, Doug greets me with a big smile and says, "We're going white-water rafting!"

We're in Jamaica. I have to admit the cruise ports all look pretty much the same. Same duty-free booze, same jewelry. This one has a bar that is maybe supposed to look like a pirate ship instead of a tiki hut, but otherwise they're all much of a muchness. And we're whisked away in a bus to wherever our excursion is starting from and then back again. It's all very sanitized. Someday I'm going to come back to these places and really explore them.

I could explore them with Doug.

No. Not going there. I'm not letting myself wallow in maybes today.

Except Doug is making it really hard.

I'm very aware that the whole "let's pretend to be married" thing was my idea, and Doug's personality has meant I'm the one to start most conversations. If our relationship was real, I'd think we were figuring out our schtick. Every couple has one. But since we aren't, and since I'm trying to give myself some breathing room, I figure I'll just hang back a bit. Today our schtick will be the quiet gays who keep to themselves. Less chance of getting myself in trouble that way.

What I don't anticipate is Doug stepping into the void.

Pure luck has us sitting on the bus next to a family from Toronto, and as soon as they find out Doug—and now me, as Doug tells them excitedly—is from Toronto too, everyone is best friends. They compare notes, and it turns out the family—a husband and wife and their two teenage kids—only lives ten minutes away from where *we* live.

"Isn't that a hilarious coincidence?" Doug gives me a bright smile.

"Sure is, my little butter dish." Butter dish? Even I know that one was bad.

He pats my thigh, his hand warm and higher up than is strictly appropriate in mixed company. I don't know if it's intentional or if he's just excited, because he and the family talk about their favourite places to eat and complain about Toronto traffic, but the brush of his fingers has my cock twitching, and it short-circuits my brain, so all I can do is smile and nod.

The family is full of staunch hockey fans. We, apparently, love basketball.

"We went to our first Raptors game last year. Now we're just the biggest Raptor fans, aren't we, honey?" Doug's hand has moved to my back, and his thumb sweeps over the nape of my neck, making me shiver.

I don't understand what's going on. He was distraught last night, and now he's every inch the doe-eyed newlywed. He can't go more than a few seconds without touching me. Once, in a quiet moment as the bus rolls down the highway, he drops his chin to my shoulder, his breath washing over my skin like a hurricane, making me jerk.

"You okay?" he asks, his hand on my cheek like he's checking for a fever. I simultaneously want to nuzzle into the touch and shove it away, because I am so confused.

I kissed him and he ran away. He might still be in love with his fiancé, and yet he's touching me like a lover.

I can't make myself ask him what's going on, because just the idea of saying the words immediately brings to mind the sad, hesitant face I've seen so many times. So I smile and nod some more, dooming myself to whatever game he's playing.

Even though I expect him to be nervous about the rafting, like he was with snorkelling, Doug's step has a definite spring as he gets off the bus.

"Have you done this before?" I ask.

"No. But they have safety gear for us. How bad can it be?"

It may be safe, but it sure ain't sexy. They wrap us up in hideous yellow lifejackets and bright orange helmets. I look like a worn-out crayon. But Doug doesn't seem to care as he bumps his shoulder against mine. "Ready to go?"

I laugh, despite everything. "You're in a good mood today."

He shrugs. "I guess so."

"Any reason in particular?"

Doug tugs on the helmet strap under his chin, settling it against his beard. "Not really. I just figured we're halfway through this trip, and I should stop worrying."

My skin prickles with little icy sparks. I can't decide if he means worrying about rafting or what will happen with Calvin when he goes home.

The raft is a big inflatable blue thing. The family from Toronto gets on with us—the teenagers in the front row, their parents behind us once the guide says the back is the safest place to be. Doug may be putting on a brave face, but the mother has clearly been talked into this excursion by her husband and kids and insists she wants to sit in the back.

The first ten minutes take us down a murky green river. The water is flowing but hardly what I'd call white. I've canoed on rivers that move faster than this. The guide is giving us pointers on how to paddle and what to do if someone falls out, although his technique on this last part seems to mostly consist of "hope and float."

The first rapid is around a bend. It reminds me of the baby roller coasters you see at summer carnivals. A few good bumps, the kids in front of us laugh as water splashes their faces and their mother shrieks behind us, and we're through.

Doug's face is bright and excited, and even in the unflattering life jacket and boxy helmet, he's so handsome. His smile is wide, and for a second, I can see how he was last night, proud and confident as he kicked trivia butt, before everything got confusing again.

I don't have much time to think about it, though, because the water is moving faster now, and as we come around another curve, the river drops out from underneath the boat. We follow a split second later. The rapid is loud, and it seems to be trying to twist the raft so we go through sideways. The guide shouts at us to paddle, and I do. The kids in front of us hoot, and Doug laughs beside me as the water splashes over the sides, soaking our feet.

"Everyone all right?" the guide asks when we're through. The kids are paddling furiously towards the next set of rapids. Doug joins them. His arms bulge, and I'm so mesmerized by the straining effort that it's only when the guide calls to start paddling again that I tear my eyes away.

The third one is big. And has a rock in the middle. It's a lot like a roller coaster, but one of the big ones. The kind where they strap you in and triple-check you won't go flying as it careens around, except there are no straps in the raft. I wedge my feet under the rubbery seat the kids in front of us are sitting on. I glance at Doug, but he's got his game face on again, and holy shit, that look really does it for me.

But I can't watch for long as the raft veers to one side and I'm nearly knocked overboard. We hit a wave side-on, and my head is submerged as a wall of water crashes over us. It feels like my helmet is being sucked off, and I brace my legs as I grip the side of the raft. When the rapid releases me, I pop back up like a demented jack-in-the-box, but I can't help my shouted laughter.

"That was amazing! Oh my God! Dougie, did you—"

The words die as I turn my head to tell my imaginary husband about my dunking only to discover he really must be imaginary, because he isn't there.

"Doug?"

Another rush of water crashes over my head, and when my vision clears, I catch a glimpse of a helmet and then Doug's face, bobbing in the rapids, before it disappears under the foam.

"He's over there!" I point like an explorer searching for land. "We have to go get him."

The guide laughs behind me, the raft small enough that I can hear it over the roar of the water. "Nah. We can't fight the rapid. Keep paddling! We'll pick him up when we're through this."

"But—" I've lost track of Doug, and my heart is in my throat. While the family around me keeps paddling gamely like nothing is wrong, I search desperately for Doug. He's not a good swimmer. He was so nervous yesterday. The raft pitches again, and I'm so scared for him I can barely get my arms to move as I try to help out with the paddling and get us out of here.

It's over in seconds, and as soon as the river calms, I'm half standing, looking for any sign of him, ignoring the guide as he tells me to sit down.

"Doug!" I shout.

I scream when a wet hand grabs mine against the side of the raft. I don't know what I'm expecting—some Jamaican siren ready to drag me to my death, maybe—but I nearly faint with shock when I see Doug's glowing face staring up at me from the water.

"Oh! Oh, honey!" I scramble for him, nearly falling out of the raft. "Are you okay?" My hands tangle in his, and I try to pull him in, but I'm shaking and he's heavy, and it's only when the man behind me reaches over and grabs the neck of Doug's life jacket that we manage to get his chest and shoulders over the side, so he can kick and wiggle his way back into the raft.

I fall backwards, and he lands on top of me. I'm still talking. "Are you okay? Are you hurt? You don't like to swim. Oh, sugar bear, I was so scared."

He's breathless and laughing as he sits up, pulling me with him. I can't help myself. I haven't even let him speak, but my words are coming out in a rush, like the rapid we're still gliding away from, and when I finally realize everyone is staring, all I can think to do is stop my words with his mouth.

My kisses are rough, frantic, and he's laughing and telling me he's fine. I throw my arms around his shoulders and hold him close.

"I'm okay, Tripp," he says softly in my ear, making me shudder. I don't know why I'm so emotional about this, but the moment I looked and Doug wasn't in the raft was one of the most terrifying of my life.

"How come you don't kiss me like that?" the man behind us asks.

"They're newlyweds," his wife says. "We kissed like that sixteen years ago."

————

We stop for lunch on a rocky beach. A crew is waiting for us, along with the other groups of rafters. Picnic benches have been set up, and I don't even want to think about how they got here, but Doug and I find a flat rock and sit, shoulder to shoulder, and eat in silence.

"Are you having fun?" Doug asks.

"Apart from when you almost drowned, yes."

He bumps his shoulder against mine. "I'm fine. It was scary at first, but once I realized the life jacket was going to keep me floating, I just focused on not bouncing off the rocks."

If his words are supposed to make me feel better, they don't. He must see it on my face, because he puts his plastic fork down and turns towards me, one hand on my cheek so I have to look at him.

His kiss is soft and slow, and even though we're surrounded by chatty tourists and perky staff, I feel like we're the only two people here.

I don't want to open my eyes as he pulls away, so the most immediate sensation isn't the image of his face or the brightness of the sun. It's the tickle of his beard on my cheek. He brushes it, up and down, over my skin a few times, and the rasp calms me, centers me.

"I'm okay. You don't have to worry. I'm not worried."

"You're not?" I suddenly realize how—actually—worried I am. I have been since he fell asleep in my arms last night and I spent hours trying to figure out how this adventure has a happy ending.

"No. Just like the rapids. I have everything I need to be okay. Now I'm ready to see how it plays out."

It sounds so brave and so terrifying. "You're just going to hope and float?"

He kisses me again. I can't get enough of him when he kisses me. "I might kick a little, just to see if I can get myself headed in the right direction."

I really hope we're both paddling together for the rest of this trip.

13

DOUG

I really hope Tripp gets what I mean. It's not about falling out of the raft. I could have done without that. But I wasted yesterday evening worrying about things I can't control and more things that might not happen—and I'm not even sure I want to happen.

I like who I am with Tripp. And the longer I'm with him, the more I realize I don't like who I'd become with Calvin.

It's complicated, of course, because so much of my relationship is tied up in months of grief after my dad died, but somehow, in the process, I'd given up control. At first it was necessary. I'd have starved to death or developed a million health complications by living on takeout if Calvin hadn't been there to buy groceries. But it's been almost a year since he proposed and two years since my dad died. The initial shock and grief stopped ages ago. I'll always be sad, but that debilitating feeling of loss has been gone for so long I don't remember when it changed.

And still I let Calvin treat me like a child, because it was easier. Because on the rare moments I tried to reassert myself, he'd smile and tell me not to worry.

"No, baby, I'll take care of it. You just take care of yourself."

He said that about everything. From the wedding to paying bills to picking a movie to watch on a Friday night.

I organize a freaking film festival, and somehow I fell into a pattern where my boyfriend was the one to choose the movies.

Tripp is extra attentive for the rest of the afternoon—or as attentive as one can be in a rubber raft. I don't fall out again, and we're both wet and tired—so tired we fall asleep head to head on the bus ride back—as we make our way onto the ship. We're quiet in the long hall back to the suite, and I nearly pass the grinning leprechaun before Tripp catches my hands and pulls me back.

"Want the first shower?" I ask.

He gives me a soft smile. "That would be nice."

I only mean to lie down long enough to relax and wait for my turn in the shower, but the next thing I know, Tripp's shaking me awake.

"Hey. Supper's in ten minutes."

I've been so dead to the world I need a second to understand what he's said, and when the words register, I bounce out of bed.

"What? Ten minutes! Why didn't you wake me up sooner?"

He shrugs. "I figured you could use the sleep."

"But we missed the whole afternoon!" I don't know what I thought I was going to do with the hours between leaving Jamaica and our dinner time. In my head, it involved kissing without an audience, but that was about as specific as it got.

Like he can read my mind, Tripp leans in and kisses me once. "We'll just have to stay up late."

I hope he knows how tempting that sounds.

Dinner is in the main dining room. I like it there best. I booked all the fancy restaurants for Calvin, because I knew he'd want to try them, but any place that has Caesar salad and prime rib on the menu every night is okay by me.

When the server comes to ask about dessert, he mentions they have a special that night on fortified wines. I'm not much of a wine drinker. I know I like red better than white, but if you ask me the difference between a merlot and a cabernet, I'll tell you one has more letters. But Tripp looks excited.

"Have you ever tried port?" he asks. When I shake my head, he orders two.

They come in tiny glasses. Calvin took me to Niagara-on-the-Lake once for an ice wine tasting. They served the wine there in small glasses like these. When I taste the port, it's syrupy and thick on my tongue, and I roll it around for a minute. I almost expect it to taste like cough syrup—it has that kind of consistency—but the bitter medicinal flavour never comes.

"Well?" Tripp asks.

I think about it. In Niagara, Calvin used words like apricot and peach, vanilla and honey. What does this taste like?

"It reminds me of the raisins you used to get in little boxes for snacks in kindergarten."

He laughs, but somehow with Tripp, I never get the feeling he's laughing at me.

I pause as a thought occurs to me. "What's your real name?"

His laughter fades. "What?"

"Last night, you said Tripp was a nickname for a son with the same name as his father and grandfather. So what's your real name?"

"Tripp's my real name."

"It's what's on your birth certificate?"

"No." He takes another sip of his port. "But it's what I've always used. Seriously. My whole life. I don't think anyone has ever called me—" He inhales sharply.

"Come on. It's not actually Chet, is it?" I slide my hand over the table until it touches his. He doesn't resist when I mesh our fingers together and stroke my thumb over his skin. "You can tell me."

He's blushing. He's totally blushing. Tripp is the one with the plan, the one who can chat with anyone and make them believe he's the doting husband who moved across the country to be with his one true love—even if it's only me—and now I've made him blush.

This is even better than winning at trivia.

"It's Emerson," he says.

I snort, but his face is pinched, like he's annoyed to have told me, so I smother it before it becomes a full-blown laugh. "That's —um—I don't think I've ever met an Emerson before. It's very—"

"Stuffy? Pretentious? It gets worse. My middle name is Gabriel." He sighs heavily.

"Emerson Gabriel Gillingham III." I roll it around on my tongue, like the port. It leaves the same sticky residue. "Not as stuffy as Chet-Bryson Gillingham-Freeman, but it's getting there. And your dad was—"

"My dad goes by Gabe. My grandfather went by Emerson. And I have always been Tripp." His gaze is steady now, like he's daring me to call him anything else. I want to. He has all these pet names for me. Surely he'll let me call him Em or something? I don't like Gabe. He doesn't look like a Gabe.

No, he looks like a Tripp. Bright eyes, sharp features, and blond hair that never sits quite flat on his head.

My Tripp. That's who he looks like.

As we leave the dining room, I'm feeling very awake, despite the day of rafting. Must be the nap. Either way, my steps bounce as I ask, "What should we do now?"

Tripp shrugs. "What do you feel like doing?"

Despite my growing conviction, I'm still not brave enough to say what I really want, so instead I say, "There's a foam party at the indoor pool?" I'd seen it on the daily agenda and dismissed it, but since we can't have trivia every night, it seems like the best available option.

"A foam party?" He laughs. "What are we, twenty-one?"

"The average age on this ship has to be at least sixty. We're a couple young bucks by comparison."

"No one under the age of fifty says 'young buck.'"

"Well, what do you want to do?" I ask, annoyed he's not playing along, but my annoyance vanishes under the arch of Tripp's eyebrow and the way his bottom lip disappears beneath a tooth as he looks me up and down.

Yes. Yes. With Tripp, I feel braver than I have in a long time, but still not that brave. If anything is going to happen, I need him to make the first move.

I can't decide if I'm relieved or disappointed when he says, "Foam party it is!"

We detour to change back into trunks and T-shirts.

The indoor pool has been transformed from a spa-like oasis to a dimly lit discotheque. Laser lights bounce off the walls while smoke machines send white tendrils billowing around our ankles. The party is well under way as we walk in, and people are bobbing in the pool up to their necks in foam that floats along the surface of the water. Music thumps with a deep bass, and people not interested in the bubble bath are dancing along the pool deck, while cruise staff hands out glowing necklaces. Tripp takes two and puts his on before he slips the other one around my neck. His smile is bright as he steps back.

"It suits you."

"Luminescent green?"

He snags a finger in it, pulling just firmly enough that I take a step forwards but not so hard it pops off. "If you don't like it, we can give it to the leprechaun on the way back to our room."

Our room. Ours. I lick my lips at how he says it. Easy. Casual.

"Should we get in?" I ask, feeling not so casual. As I speak, a cascade of foam pours out of the machine at the far end, and the people in the water squeal and throw their hands up as they're engulfed by the bubbly tidal wave.

The pool seems to be a single depth from one side to the

other. Tripp and I peel off our shirts and climb in. The water is warm, and the foam is vaguely strawberry-scented. I'm submerged halfway up my chest, but the waves of foam mean that sometimes I'm covered to my chin.

Tripp finds my hand and pulls me farther out into open water. The pool isn't as big as the outdoor ones but still wide enough we can make our way towards the middle without bumping into too many people. They've set the lights along the edge of the pool—just below the water—to slowly move from blue to purple to green, while the thin lights overhead wheel in wild patterns, bouncing in a million directions where they hit the bubbles.

"It's kind of like the tamest rave you've ever been to, isn't it?" Tripp asks.

"You think I've ever been to a rave?"

He laughs, stepping closer to me. "No, I think you're way more of a Netflix-and-chill kind of guy."

I blush. I'm into Netflix and chill only in the literal sense. Homebody. Calvin used to call me that, and never like it was a good thing.

"More like Netflix and cheese pizza," I say.

His kiss is gentle, just a soft press of lips on mine while his arms drape over my shoulders. The contact is electric, like the sparks of light bouncing off the foam around us.

"You're way more than cheese pizza," he says.

Dancing in a pool is weird. The water means we can't really do more than shuffle if we don't want to splash the people closest to us, but at the same time, the bubbles create these little pockets, insulating us from the others. The glow from our plastic necklaces reflect off the honeycomb of foam at our shoulders.

We stay like that for a long time. His arms around me, our faces close but not touching, listening quietly as the cruise staff whoops and cheers and tells us to do things like get the party started and put our hands up.

"I'm really glad you didn't drown today," Tripp says out of nowhere.

I laugh, pressing my hands against his hips. "I don't think there was ever a chance of that." It all happened really fast. One second, I was paddling, and the next thing I knew, the raft hit a bump and I was in the river. But even when I should have been scared, I just kept my feet pointed downriver and my eye on the raft. The first person I saw when I got close was Tripp, and I reached for his hand. "I knew you'd help me."

His kiss is less gentle this time, tongue pushing against my lips until I let him in. His hands slide up into my hair, holding me against him while he pours so much feeling into his mouth —like he did on the raft—that I start to feel dizzy.

"Doug," he says in my ear, voice rough. "I really like you."

"I like you too." I rub my cheek against his, and his grip tightens against my scalp. He likes my beard.

"Would it be inappropriate for me to feel you up in this pool?"

My dick, the one that betrayed me so many times in the last few months with Calvin, perks up, but my cheeks heat too. "This is technically an all-ages event." I haven't actually seen anyone here who might be younger than legal drinking age, though.

He turns me so my back is pressed to his front, and his hands hold me close, one on my chest, the other on my belly. "Perfectly PG-13," he says in my ear. "We'll just dance."

Except we're not dancing. His touch on my skin, his breath on my neck. Anyone with half a brain would know what's going on if they could see us clearly through the dim light and the bubbles. He pulls me to one side, where the foam is thicker, and we're basically hidden for a moment. His dick his getting hard. I can feel it pressing against my ass.

"Doug," he says. "I want you. I really do. I know it wasn't part of our agreement, but—"

"Yes." I press back against him. Any of the dancers nearby can see us grinding, but we won't be here much longer. "Yes. I want that too." Might need it, actually. It's been so long since I've wanted anyone, actually wanted to be a participant in anything sexual. And now that Tripp's mouth is on my back, where the hump of my spine joins my neck, I can't think of anything I want more.

Dancing like this, touching like this, is a terrifying temptation. The longer we do it, the less I care if anyone sees us. Not that I'll fuck him right here, but we're not doing anything wrong. Up on the pool deck, a guy in Hawaiian-print board shorts is dancing with a woman in a black bikini exactly the same way, and no one is saying anything to them. Why should Tripp and I feel shy?

But I want more. Dancing isn't enough. Touching isn't enough. Tripp's hand is above my belly button, and I want it lower. The hard length of him trapped between us isn't where I want it to be either. I want it in my hand. In my mouth. I want to know what he sounds like the first time I taste him.

"We should go," I say.

Tripp grips my chin to turn my head. He kisses me, hips pushing against me. "You go first. I'll be thirty seconds behind you. Just need to do some . . . deep breathing."

I laugh. Swim trunks are just about the worst thing for erections and modesty. "That'll teach you to get overexcited."

His eyes flash as I pull free of his arms. "Just you wait."

14

TRIPP

I wouldn't say I have a type. Liam was long and lean, polished and pretty. The guy I was with before him was skinny and tattooed. Before that, it was tweed and grandpa cardigans.

But tonight, my type is this:

1) The perfect outline of Doug's ass in his damp trunks.

2) The shy way he keeps checking over his shoulder as we walk down the hall, like he knows I'm staring at his ass.

3) The eagerness in his eyes as he starts pulling off his shirt before the suite door is even fully closed.

I'm not really any better. As soon as I can see the beginnings of his hairy belly, I'm on top of him, mouth on his, legs tangling together as we tumble back onto his bed. Our bed. If tonight goes the way I hope it does, I'm sleeping here for the rest of the trip.

"What do you like?" he asks, but then he's kissing me again so quickly I don't have time to get the words out. I like him. Have since the first moment I saw his sad face while I was naked and ridiculous in the hall. I like the careful way he chooses his food. I like the way he orders me breakfast even though I could live on coffee. I like how he holds my hand.

We roll so he's on top, and his hips settle between my thighs, and oh yeah, I like that too. I haven't even seen his dick yet, but just the weight of him, the way he rolls and presses into me while his tongue slips between my lips—yeah, I like all of that.

"You didn't answer my question."

I laugh, sliding a hand between our mouths so he has to stop kissing me for a second. "You wouldn't let me answer."

He smiles against my palm and my heart melts like cheap Easter chocolate.

"Sorry." The syllables are muffled, and if a human were able to make actual heart eyes, I'd be doing it right now. I'm so gone on this guy. My husband. Imaginary. Temporary. Perfect.

"I like everything." If Doug's doing it, the list of things I could object to is pretty short.

He rolls off me, onto his side, propping his head up. My erection pitches a tent in my trunks again. God, getting that thing to go down so I could actually exit the pool was the most painful exercise in willpower I have ever experienced.

"Hand jobs?"

I snort. "Perfected my technique as soon as I hit puberty."

"Blow jobs?" Doug's lower lip is full, puckered out over the soft edge of his beard. The sight of it sliding along the bottom of my dick is pretty much a perfect mental image. I can't help myself as I palm my cock to keep it from tearing through the nylon of my shorts.

Doug grins. "Do you top?"

"Bottom." I will top, but tonight I want the stretch of Doug's dick inside me more than I want the sun to come up tomorrow.

"Do you—"

"Oh, for God's sake." I groan as I struggle out of my trunks, my rock-hard erection snagging against the elastic. "If you ask me tonight, I'll cover myself in chocolate pudding and let you lick it off me while I sing 'God Save the Queen.'"

His eyes go wide, his breath catching on an inhale. Then he's laughing, a great body-shaking bellow that only lasts long enough for him to crawl out of his clothes too before he's back on top of me, trapping our dicks between us while he kisses me. His beard is a soft rasp on my cheeks, and his body is all warm heat, and I could die happy right here.

"I haven't done this in a long time," he says.

"What?" Did that asshole fiancé—"

"No, I mean, I haven't been able to. My— With the wedding stress and with— If I can't—"

Oh, holy fuck. This is a lot of responsibility. I cup his cheek. "Baby. Anything you do is going to be perfect. We can just hump against each other like high school freshman until we get bored and then watch reruns of *Downton Abbey* until we fall asleep. I will still love it."

But I would love getting fucked more.

Still, I'm sympathetic to performance issues. We've all had them from time to time, and Doug's had his fair share of stress. I can't even imagine what it must be like to lose a parent. And if Calvin ever made Doug feel bad for it for even a second, I will fly to Toronto, find him, and murder him with a paperclip.

I am going to do everything I can to make Doug feel like a king tonight.

I roll us again, so he's on his back and I'm half on top of him. My erection isn't as demanding as it was a minute ago, but I'm okay with that. We'll get there. I kiss him slow, the way I'm learning he prefers, before I let my hands go exploring. His body is broad, his chest hairy. I flick one of his nipples, watching his face for signs he likes it or doesn't care. The flicking doesn't do much for him, but pinching does. When I tug on his nipple between two fingers, he grunts in the back of his throat, and his hand tightens where he's holding on to my upper arm.

"Teeth?" I ask, and he nods, so I wriggle down until I can lick at his nipple before I take it between my teeth and pull. He lets out a long exhale that strangles itself when I let the tip of my tongue brush over the bit of his flesh trapped in my mouth.

He does the same thing when I move to the other side, shifting restlessly under me. He doesn't talk much, but that's okay. He's a wealth of hints if you just listen. I nuzzle and lick at the hair and soft skin along his ribs and under his armpit. He tastes clean, a bit like chlorine and strawberries from the pool, and as I nuzzle in, he lifts his arm over his head to give me better access. I could drown in his scent and his taste right here.

A tentative hand is moving down my body, over my side, and along my hip, and I want to scream, "Yes! Yes!" but I don't want to scare him, so I keep doing what I'm doing, licking and nipping, and very subtly—I think it's subtly, and he doesn't complain—roll my hips back so he can reach where he wants to go.

His palm is soft, but his grip says he knows what he's doing when he closes it around my dick. The first stroke is a bit tight, but he readjusts, gliding over my skin, and it's perfect.

I reach up to kiss him, and we roll together, belly to belly. His hand is trapped between us, working slowly. His thumb strokes over the head of my cock, and all the ache and need comes roaring back.

I distract myself by reaching for him too. He's half-hard, and I don't wrap my hand around him just yet, preferring instead to run my knuckles over him, giving him space to back away if he wants. But with every pass, I can feel the stutter of his hand on my dick, and slowly, his erection comes to life.

"Can I see you?" I ask.

"Do you want to?"

I wouldn't ask if I didn't. Gently, I push at his shoulder and try not to moan as he lets go of my dick to roll away. He lies there, and I'm sure he's uncomfortable, but he's also so perfect in my eyes. Thick chest. Round belly. His cock isn't as long as mine, but it's wide and it's going to feel perfect when he— "Will you fuck me?"

His eyebrows bunch together. "Can I blow you first. Just a little? I kinda like— And, sometimes, if I can't—" He licks his lips, and his hand moves nervously over his stomach.

I crawl up his whole body, kissing every inch I pass. "Anything you want, my little coconut."

He laughs, and whatever he's feeling, I'm glad he's relaxed enough he can still laugh. Sometimes half the problem with sex is people take it way too seriously, when it's really just bodies flopping around like seals and making noises your mother would tell you aren't polite at the dinner table.

There are a lot of ways to give and receive a blow job. I could lie on my back and Doug could go down on me right here. Or he could sit up by the headboard and suck me off while I kneel in front of him. We could use a chair or the edge of the bed. In the end, they all feel pretty amazing.

But my absolute favourite way to have my dick in a guy's mouth is with me standing up and him on his knees. I love the view of sliding in and out of his mouth. And it might seem like a hassle to do that, because we're already in bed and have so many possibilities available to us without having to get out of it, but Doug's eager to please, and I'm eager to let him, so I get to my feet and walk to the opposite side of the room—which is admittedly not a long walk, even in a spacious honeymoon suite—and crook my finger to him.

He gives me a blinding smile as he follows. He kisses me, and being here, naked with him, is the best thing I can imagine. And then it gets better as he slides to his knees, dragging his beard and his mouth over the whole length of me as he goes.

"Oh, sugar pie." I basically forget to breathe the first time his tongue traces the length of my dick.

He is so good at this. His mouth is the right heat, his lips have just the right amount of tension as they wrap around me, exploring the tip before moving farther down. Even his spit seems to have the right amount of slide to it, and I don't know if that's even possible, except that it is right now.

"Doug," I gasp. His head bobs, and I plant my hands against the wall, spreading my palms and fingers wide to keep from gripping his hair and forcing myself into his mouth. We're doing this in his time and in the way he likes.

I'll get bossy once I have him in my ass—the way *I* like.

He takes his time. Doug's a meticulous kind of guy. He licks and sucks, sometimes using his hands, and the tight friction of his palm, compared to the wet slide of his tongue, makes my toes curl. He presses the tip into my slit, and I can't stop the whimper that starts in my chest and becomes a sob when he sucks me down until I hit the back of his throat.

"You're good at this," I pant, and he grunts, maybe like he heard me, maybe like he's struggling to breathe, but I don't have time to wonder, because his fingers are on my balls, playing and teasing, before they spread my legs apart and slide farther back.

I can't help the way my hips kick forwards when a fingertip brushes over my hole. He pops off immediately, lips swollen and slick as he looks up at me. "Okay?"

"Uh-huh," I say, chest heaving. His timing is pretty good actually, because I'd just started to think about what Doug would look like, face tipped up while he waits for me to streak his beard with come, and if I'd kept going down that road, I wouldn't have lasted long enough to find out—at least not this time.

"Is this okay?" His finger is still between my thighs, and he slips it between my cheeks, circling like he's drawing a question mark.

"Oh yeah." I run my thumb along his pretty bottom lip, trembling when he meets it with the tip of his tongue.

"Can I keep going?" He presses the pad of his finger against my opening.

"A hundred percent yes. Kinda necessary if we're—" My heart drops and my eyes go wide. "Oh no! I don't have any lube." Liam always carried lube in his kit, and I'd been too lazy to buy any of my own before we'd left. And now—

Doug rolls up to his feet, grimacing and shaking out his legs.

"Honey," I say. "If it wasn't comfortable, you should have said something."

He kisses me. His tongue tastes faintly like me. "I didn't notice my foot was asleep until I stopped sucking you off."

Now I want to drop to *my* knees and kiss the poor foot that was sacrificed for my pleasure. Instead, I ask, "Lube?"

He grins before walking his bouncy, naked ass over to the small dresser at the foot of the bed. He stands there for a moment, hands on his hips, cock pointing at a forty-five-degree angle like a divining rod. The look on his face says he's making a tough decision, but whatever it is, he sighs, bends, and opens up the bottom drawer.

"I didn't think I'd use this, but—"

What appears next is a sex toy bonanza.

15

DOUG

I'm pretty sure the basket is from Kate, my youngest sister. She's always been the joker of the family. I mentioned my . . . problems to her once. I was so worried Calvin and I would get here and I wouldn't be able to be what he wanted. What sexually active couple wouldn't have sex on their honeymoon? Kate and I talked about toys to help, but I never worked up the courage to actually buy some. So I can only assume she arranged for the basket to be in the suite back when she thought Calvin and I might need some encouragement once we tied the knot.

Instead, it was the first thing I saw when I checked in to my room. I threw it into the bottom drawer and resigned myself to living out of my suitcase for the rest of the trip so I wouldn't have to go near it again. No doubt, in everything that happened after the wedding was called off, contacting the cruise line and asking them to remove the debauchery basket from the suite slipped her mind.

Good thing too. I've had sex before using only the lube from the condom, but it was slow and stressful to get started, and I'm pretty sure both of those factors would just end in me going limp and Tripp pretending like it's no big deal.

"My sister has no shame," I say, rifling through the basket until I find the two bottles of lube at the bottom.

"Your sister?" Tripp asks with wide eyes.

"She's a public health nurse. Nothing is off-limits for her," I say. "Do you have a preference between raspberry and vanilla?"

He wrinkles his nose, pulling out yet more stuff. "I've never understood the point of flavored lube. Why would I want to eat it when I can eat you instead?"

I blush, feeling very naked, while the images his words conjure up make my dick leak embarrassingly.

He strolls—no, he struts—up to me and holds up a line of condoms stretching from his shoulder to the floor.

"Optimistic."

Unnecessary, since Calvin and I stopped using condoms a while ago, but I don't say that. Fortuitous, now that Tripp is here with me instead.

He also pulls out a length of black silicone beads, what looks like a combination plug and cock ring, and a bright pink prostate massager.

Tripp cocks an eyebrow. "Your sister know what you like?"

I cough. "No. But that's never stopped Kate. At a family reunion last summer, my aunt was telling everyone about the Magic Bullet she got for Mother's Day, and Kate took that as an invitation to tell everyone about the new rabbit vibrator she'd just gotten too."

His shoulders shake. "Isn't a Magic Bullet a blender?"

"Kate knows her sex toys better than her kitchen appliances."

Tripp flicks on the massager, letting it vibrate gently against the tip of his finger. My cock bobs at the sight of it, and he grins. "I think he likes it."

"Uh—" is the only thing I manage to say. The options are suddenly overwhelming, and all I can think is: What if none of them work for me?

He must see the rising panic on my face, because he smiles sweetly and sets the vibe down. "We'll stick with the basics tonight. Lots of time to explore the rest."

Except there isn't lots of time. We're on the back leg of this cruise, and we're only just now getting to this point with each other. We—

"Hey." His hand is on my cheek. "It's okay. One night at a time."

We sit on the edge of the bed. Or, rather, I sit, and he crawls into my lap so we can kiss. He feels light and small in my arms, even though I'm so aware of his hard edges and tough muscles most of the time. I want to gather him up and hold on to him.

His knuckles are back on my cock, skimming, asking. Calvin stopped asking. He got impatient and gave up instead.

"Hey," Tripp says again. "I'm here. Be here with me."

I'm trying. So hard. I want to be with him for a very long time.

The lube in his palm is cool when he touches me, but his tongue in my mouth is hot and demanding, and the combination perks me up again in no time. I growl as he works me, reveling in the ache between my thighs, the need to put my cock to use when so often in the past I've—

Not thinking about that. I'm here. Tripp is here and wants me, and that's what's important.

I gather him up and roll us. He laughs as we tumble back onto the mattress, him on his back and me holding myself over him, resting on my elbows.

"I was so embarrassed the first time we met," he says.

"Because you were naked?"

"Because you were hot and I was naked." He runs his hands over my chest.

I've never been thin. In college I was the friendly fat guy. No one I've ever slept with has ever complained about my body, but no one has ever called me hot either.

I find his cock straining against mine and grip them together. Mine is still slick, and he cries out as they roll in my palm.

"Yes. Yes, please, Dougie. I need you."

He does. I want to believe he does, at any rate. Because if he needs me, then maybe he'll stay. And the more time we spend together, the more I think I want to be with him, even when we're back to our normal lives.

"You feel amazing," I say. He's hard and hot and glides against me like we were made to be together.

"Fuck me," he says, widening his knees. "Please, I don't want to come until you fuck me."

I kiss him, suck on his skin just below his collarbone. He moans and holds my head there, so I keep sucking until he's red and swollen, marked for anyone to see. And people *will* see. If there's one place it's acceptable to be shirtless and show off your hickeys, surely it's a cruise ship.

"Doug," he whines, and I can't keep him waiting anymore. I shimmy down, sliding between his legs, while he lifts his feet and pulls his knees up against his chest.

"Show me."

He does. Grips his cheeks and spreads himself apart for my inspection. He's pretty and perfect. Pink with little swirls of hair that some guys don't like but I appreciate. It makes him seem real, when everything that has happened to us is endlessly surreal.

I run a finger over the tight muscle, and he jerks like I've bitten him.

"Okay?" I ask, running my hands over the back of his thighs.

"Yes." He pants. "Just excited."

"Raspberry or vanilla?"

"Oh fuck, I don't care, just—" He chokes off when I press one finger against him. I haven't grabbed the lube yet, so I don't do more than catch the tip of one nail against his entrance, but he hisses and rocks back farther, exposing himself more.

"Vanilla. Use the vanilla. It's closer. Raspberry's still on the dresser."

An excellent reason. I grab the bottle and drizzle a little over his crack, enjoying the way he jerks and squeaks as it drips over his skin.

"More." His teeth are clenched. "More, more, Dougie, please."

I'm not inside of him. Not even a knuckle. "You gonna make it?"

He nods frantically. "I just want you. Please."

His excitement demands a faster pace than I might normally like, but one I find I'm comfortable with. I work him open with my fingers until he's rocking against my hand, fucking himself while he babbles my name and calls me silly things like "fuzzy bunny" and "plum tart." I watch the way his skin turns pink and then bright red, even under his immaculate tan. My cock is hard and leaking, but I could watch him do this until he comes and be satisfied.

Except he still wants more. My husband is so greedy. I can't even describe what it feels like—the gleam in his eyes as his hips rock and he stares at me, begging me to get inside him.

I can do this. Maybe the strip of condoms isn't so optimistic after all.

Tripp grumbles like a dog whose nap has been interrupted when I pull my fingers out so I can get the condom on. But when I'm gloved and slicked, he's back to lifting his knees apart immediately, pulling his ass up and waiting impatiently.

I line myself up, and I half expect him to slam down, rolling onto me like he can't possibly wait a minute longer, but the second I start to push inside, he stills. His eyes go wide, and his breath turns shallow.

His body is a tight, welcoming haven, and I slide in like I've been here a hundred times before. Everything about it, from his long happy sigh to the way his thighs cradle my hips, just feels right.

When our pelvises meet and I can't go in any farther, I wait, adjusting to the position and the knowledge that I've crossed a line. Sex doesn't always have to be some magical coming together, but I haven't had sex with anyone not-Calvin in years, and now I've done it and it felt easy.

He licks his lips, eyes on mine, like he knows what I'm thinking. He always knows what I'm thinking. "You okay?"

I nod, bringing myself fully to the man spread out beneath me, who wants me, all of me, and who I want too, maybe more than I've ever wanted anyone, including the man I thought I would spend my life with.

I reach around me, find the little vanilla bottle, and squirt some in my hand. A few quick pulls on Tripp's cock and he's shuddering. I haven't even started moving, and his knees are already tight against my ribs. He palms my shoulders, and I let him pull me down, releasing his dick so I can brace myself on either side of his head. I kiss him, tasting salt and saliva, and then I rock my hips back, slow. So slow.

"Doug." He moans, the pitch going high in anticipation, fingernails digging into my skin as I pull back, to just the tip, and plunge back into him again.

We do that for a long time. His body is hot and slick, and the space between us gets slippery with sweat, but I can't get enough of the way he whines and writhes while I push myself into him over and over. I thought it would be strange, that I'd hesitate or wait for him to take control. But every sound he makes as he throws his head back for me to suck on the tender spot at the bottom of his throat says I have it exactly right, and the only thing I know to do with that information is to keep going.

"Doug. Doug. Doug," he chants in time with my thrusts. "Doug. Gonna. Gonna. Gon—" He arches, and I don't even have time to help stroke him off before the hot spurt between us says he's coming, and I didn't need to do anything besides fuck him.

I slide my hands around his body instead, under his back and over his shoulders, so that I can control every inch of his movement. I mash our lips together, and he moans as I pump into him. His ass is so tight now, flexing and spasming, and with every thrust, I fight for another fraction of an inch, another second of friction, to get me where I need to go.

"You're so hot," he says, voice ragged in my ear. "Such a god right now. Fill me. Make me yours." His nails scratch on my skin, and the pressure in my balls is too much to ignore, and I erupt. It's like an earthquake that starts in the small of my back and shakes me apart, one bone at a time, while I empty myself over and over into the latex I wish wasn't there. I don't want anything between us. Not a condom. Not Calvin. Nothing.

I more or less collapse on him. I've been so careful, but my body is officially done. They don't call it a release for nothing. Tripp's breaths are loud in my ear, and he heaves underneath me, not to escape, but to gasp back to consciousness the way I'm doing.

"Wow," I say.

"Yeah." His hands are still moving over my skin. My fingers and toes are tingling.

"Good thing we've got extra condoms," he says. "I may never get out of this bed again."

16

TRIPP

I remember three things about that night we have sex the first time.

After an hour of sleeping in sweat and spunk-scented sheets, we realize we have a perfectly clean pull-out couch not ten feet away. We tumble into it and promptly fall asleep again.

About an hour after that, I wake up to find I have fallen asleep on my arm and it is so deeply numb I can't move it. When I try, I only succeed in smacking myself in the face.

A few hours later, before the sun comes up, I wake again. Doug and I have rolled to face each other. We're nose to nose, and normally I hate being breathed on in my sleep, but the tickle of his beard makes me smile. One of his arms is thrown over my hip, and our legs are tangled together. Even our dicks— mine still free and loose, his snugged up in his briefs but defi- nitely awake—are pointing towards each other, like little dick magnets trying to find true north.

I should help them out.

I shimmy forwards. Doug's hand slides farther, until the tips of his fingers are brushing my ass. My ass is sore. He was as thick as I thought he'd be, but I didn't foresee him being so strong. He

133

needed no coaxing at all once he was in, and holy mother Mary on a cracker, was I there for that.

I brush my lips over his, and his nose wrinkles. When I flick a thumb over one bare nipple, his brows furrow. And when I press my growing cock into the crook of his hip, he inhales slowly and says, "Is it time to get up already?"

He's half-hard as I reach into his underwear, and his hips roll towards me as I squeeze.

"Yeah, baby," I say against his mouth. "Get up for me."

So none of our sheets are particularly clean by the time the *bong bong* sounds and breakfast is delivered, and it turns out I really like a few slices of melon and maybe a piece of toast in the morning. The coffee doesn't sit so acidly in my stomach with it.

Or maybe it's the company.

A man who has sex with Doug's intensity, while also showing me his kind heart, is definitely a man I want to keep around. But even as he carefully picks the seeds out of his watermelon, all I can hear is Pierce's voice in my head telling me not to fall for someone on this cruise. That it will only end in heartbreak, and I can't keep repeating old patterns. And everything is stacked against me and Doug, from how far apart we live in reality, to my habit of falling before I even know someone, to the fiancé who broke his heart but still has a claim on it. We have two full days left, and then we go back to our respective homes, and I feel sick at the thought that Doug's life probably doesn't have a place for me in it.

He's here now, though. My husband for a few more days.

"So, what's on the itinerary for today, captain?"

He breathes in his coffee slowly and gives me a smile that makes my heart stop. "We're in Haiti today. I rented us a cabana."

He didn't. He rented a cabana for *him*. The asshole. But he's long gone now. In a different climate and a different country. He had his chance, and he blew it. I've seen the way Doug's smiles have changed over the last few days. The way the sadness isn't there as much. He's going to be okay, and I'm helping him get there.

So it's our cabana.

I pack a bag to take with us while Doug's in the shower.

"What's that?" he asks as he exits the bathroom, pink and steamy.

"Just some day-trip things. Sunscreen. Your hat. A few bottles of water."

"I'm sure they'll have bottles of water there."

I kiss him, long enough that I feel the questions leave him, which is exactly what I want.

Our last stop is a private resort. The pre-fab cruise port is absent. Maybe it's a whole pre-fab island. Haiti's history hasn't exactly been conducive to making it a popular tourist destination—what with the years of colonialism, political corruption, and natural disasters. They've had other things to worry about. Yet today's stop is basically an outdoor theme park, with secluded beaches, a zip line, water trampolines for the kids, and kayaks for the whole family. It's all so sanitized.

We follow signs, Doug forging the way like an experienced tour guide. Cabana nine is the last one in the row, built slightly up on a hill. It faces a small white-sand beach that a blue-shirted attendant assures is only for us.

Good. Privacy is exactly what I'm after today.

The attendant shows us where the towels are kept. A fridge full of water—Doug gives me a raised eyebrow, but I humour him. And a simple bathroom with a pull-chain shower ("to wash the sand off" apparently). Two hammocks are strung out on a long porch, and a winding wooden staircase takes us down to the beach.

Doug is standing on the porch, trunks slung low on his hips. He leans into me as I rest my chin on his shoulder and wrap my arms around him, kissing the side of his neck.

"So what do you want to do first?" I ask.

He presses back against me, ass into my groin, one hand against my cheek. "Whatever you want to do."

We have all day. No need to rush things.

"Let's go for a swim."

Not all the cabanas around us have been rented. A couple cuddles in one of the hammocks we pass on the staircase, and a woman is lounging on a long chair on the beach, but other than that, we're alone. The beach is shallow, and we have to go out pretty far before the water is deep enough to just bob. The sun is high and hot, making me squint.

Doug swims up behind me, low in the water, just his nose and eyes exposed. He's got great eyes. A blue that looks green today. He puts one hand to my chest, and I hiss when he brushes over the giant purple hickey he sucked there last night. I did not object at the time, but I'm feeling indignant about it now.

"Troublemaker," I mutter.

He gives me half a smile but doesn't put much effort into it, and I understand why when he says, "So, tomorrow—"

"No. No." I put a finger to his lips. "Let's not do that."

He frowns. "Do what?"

"Make plans. Talk about the future. It's so complicated it makes my head hurt." And my heart. If the answer is we have no future, I'm increasingly unsure how my heart will handle that. So, instead, I wrap my arms around his shoulders and my legs around his hips, and I kiss him, long and hard. "I want today to be about us. This. The great Gillingham-Freeman-Freeman-Gillingham adventure. Let's talk about what happens later . . . well . . . later." It's too big. Too complicated, and so much of it depends on how Doug feels about a man I've never met but who should be here with him right now. It's not something we can resolve by swapping email addresses and talking about frequent flyer points as a way to make long distance work.

He doesn't look happy, but he says, "Okay." Then his knees

collapse, and he dunks us both. I come up sputtering, and he's laughing, and when I splash a handful of water towards him, he dives under and comes up a few feet away, swimming farther out into open water.

I watch him go, happy to see him relaxed. I know what he's thinking about, know what he wanted to say. But I'm not ready. I may never pack up my belongings and fly across the country to be with my one true love, and the real truth is I shouldn't, not yet, because it's what I do every time I meet someone. Maybe not across the country but across the city. One neighbourhood to the next, one lease to the next, and it has never worked well for me. So even though every inch of me says that the sweet man currently backstroking his away over a turquoise-blue ocean is the man I am meant to be with, a little voice in my head argues I can't possibly know that yet, and if I jump in and I'm wrong, I'll hurt him, and I can't have that.

But, as I head back up to the cabana, I can still feel him in my body, still taste him on my tongue, and selfish jerk that I am, I cannot make myself give those things up yet. Not today.

I'm dozing in the hammock by the time he comes back, rubbing his head with a towel.

"You tired?" he asks with a grin.

I lift my sunglasses from my face to give him my most aggrieved glare. "Someone kept me up late."

He pouts. Fucking pouts. I remember the sight of that lower lip as it slid back and forth on me last night, and even though I'm supposed to be playing the exhausted lover, my dick did not get the memo and is stirring like he wants to know what all the commotion is about.

But I have a plan, and it does not involve him. Not just yet, anyway.

"You hungry?" I ask.

"I could eat."

"Well, let's get that done with." I swing my legs over the side of the hammock.

"Before what?"

I can't help but tweak his nose. "You'll see, my darling Hufflepuff."

We order burgers and roasted corn. It's simple and delicious, and when the attendant has whisked our empty plates away, I stretch and yawn before making my way to the front of the cabana and pulling the cord I noticed earlier. It releases long panels of gauzy curtain that flutter lazily in the breeze before they settle.

Doug's lying back on the cabana's daybed, propped up on his elbows. He arches an eyebrow when I turn back to him. "Sun in your eyes?"

"Something like that. Just thought we could use a little privacy."

He licks his bottom lip. "What for?"

"I think you know." I crawl into his lap. His skin is cool against mine, and perspiration makes the hair at his temples glisten.

I'm going to make him sweat all right.

I distract him with a kiss, going for tongue because I like the rumbly sound he makes when my tongue touches his. But as his big hands come around and press into my back, I reach behind him to grab the canvas bag I filled while he was in the shower this morning.

Doug turns his head as I set the bag down. Its contents rattle.

"What's in there?"

He knows. He knows I know he knows. I know he—anyway. I pull the zipper open slowly. "We're going to play a game."

17

DOUG

I hadn't given the bag much thought. He said it was sunscreen, and sunscreen is important. But I don't have time to be annoyed at the realization that now we don't have any sunscreen, because he tips the bag over on the daybed, and I'm inundated with multicoloured sexual paraphernalia, some of which I didn't even notice last night.

Tripp stands there looking proud with his hands on his hips. "Take your pick."

I was warm already, but suddenly I'm hot. Sweat forms under my arms, while heat pools low in my belly. "What for?"

He grabs a bright green dildo, hefting it in his hand. "Looks like our leprechaun friend across the hall."

I'm tempted to make the obvious joke about keeping his hands off my lucky charms, but the way he runs a fingertip over the green silicone is distracting. My dick starts to swell, eager to go again. I haven't had sex three times in twenty-four hours in . . . well . . . ever.

The gleam in his eyes is making me nervous, though. "You pick."

He lifts the beads. They're black and a bit flexible when he

139

pushes on them. I swallow hard. He shakes his head. "Not for you, I don't think."

I don't even get a chance to react as he lifts the combination cock ring and plug. "I'm saving this one for me." A flush spreads over my chest at the thought. He winks. "Soon, my little clover leaf."

My gaze strays to the masturbator, and when I glance back at Tripp, his eyes are twinkling. "I think he likes it. You ever tried one before?"

I shake my head. "My hand works fine."

He makes a sad face again. "You deserve more than fine."

Tripp loads everything else back in the bag. I notice he leaves the ring and plug contraption at the top. Then he's back in my lap, kissing me for all he's worth and grinding against my hip, so I have no doubt where we're going.

In no time, and despite my own lingering surprise, I'm hard again, and he pushes me back. The daybed has a small mountain of pillows, and while I go about arranging them so I can sit up enough to see what he's doing, Tripp is quick about stripping off my trunks. When I eye his speedo, though, he shakes his head. "I'm still recovering from last night. Keeping mine on buys me a little more time."

So I lie there, naked and hard, wondering if he likes what he sees, or even *what* he sees, while Tripp pats his belly and sighs heavily, frowning like he can't quite remember what he's supposed to be doing. He slaps my hand away when I go to stroke myself, though, so it must be part of his game.

"Hold still," he says. Following the order is harder than it sounds, because the next thing I know, he squirts a stream of lube into his palm and then grips me. I yelp at the cool slick of his grip.

"Holy shit! You couldn't warm it up a little?" But he only needs a few quick strokes before the lube heats up with the friction, making me squirm. He doesn't go long enough to really rile me up, but I still growl when he stops.

"You're almost ready," he says with a smile. He's lubing up the sleeve, but when my hands creep towards my cock again, he scowls. I bite my lip to keep from laughing, but the laughter dies at the first gentle pressure as he places the toy over my tip. "You sure you've never used one of these before?"

I shrug. I'm not fancy like that. Being a late bloomer in every way that counted, by the time I got to college, I was good to go with my hand, some lube, and a couple pictures from the internet.

But I don't have time to think about furtive nights spent masturbating to pictures of Christian Bale in his Batman era—seriously, he was so handsome in those—before I'm engulfed in the tight grip as Tripp slides the toy down my shaft.

"Oh, God." I gasp.

"Nope. Just me, honey bear."

The squeezing suction is amazing. Not quite the same as being inside someone, but still satisfying enough that I'm gripping the sheets before I can help myself.

"So here's how it's going to work." Tripp has settled next to me, head propped in one hand, while he works the toy with the other. "This isn't about getting me off or turning me on—although it totally will anyway. But that's not your job. I just want you to feel, okay?"

"Feel what?" I arch as he slides the sleeve up and down a few more times. He leans forwards to kiss me, and I chase his lips when he rises up, then I flop back down again, all my brain cells cascading to my dick as he pumps the toy. It's so hot and tight. The inside of my chest swirls like a school of fish trying to go in a million directions at once.

Tripp says, "I'll keep going like this for a while, and then I'll speed up when I think you're ready."

"That's not much of a game."

"You didn't let me finish." He glides to a near halt, moving so slow the tension spills over my thighs and down my legs until my toes tingle. "I only want you to feel. Don't worry about me. But also, I want it to last, so while I'm doing this, you need to tell me a story."

"Goldilocks and the Three Bears?"

His laugh is soft as his lashes drop and his teeth catch his lip. "You are just right the way you are. But no, not Goldilocks and the Three Bears. I want to know about you."

"Me?"

"Yes." His hand starts moving again, distracting me just as I was about to ask what he wanted to know. This morning, he didn't want to talk about what happens next. We're less than forty-eight hours from returning to Florida, and he said he didn't want to get personal. But now he wants to know about me?

"And if I don't?"

He grins as he pulls the sleeve off, and I hiss as the air hits my cock. "Then we stop." He pushes down again, and I tense as I fight the urge to push up into the toy. "Or if you stop talking for any reason, then I'll stop too. Deal?"

"Why?"

He doesn't explain, but his smile is so open and generous. He's not playing a game, not really. He's doing this for me. Not to make me better or to fix me. This is about me and my pleasure. If I say no, I'm confident we could be napping or swimming in five minutes. If I say yes, though, he will do this for me, because he wants me to feel good.

I eye him, feeling a bit like a science experiment. "Do you play this game a lot?" I don't know why the idea makes me uncomfortable. Seven days ago, we didn't even know the other person existed. Why should I be jealous if he's used this to get to know other boyfriends?

"Never. Only you, Doug."

I like it when he says my name. I like his pet names too.

They're silly and sweet and somehow not patronizing, unlike the way Calvin always said *babe* or *sweetie* like he was talking to a pet or a child. But I like it when Tripp says my name. Like he knows me. Sees me.

"Okay." My cock thickens at my agreement, like it knows what's coming. Tripp's still moving up and down. "My dad was the first person I told I was gay."

As far as sexy game stories go, it's not a great one. Thinking about my dad does not put me in the right mood. But I really did come out to my dad before anyone else. Tripp listens intently, cheek on my shoulder.

And the story evolves, since I told my dad I was gay, in part, because I really wanted to take Eliot Greenburg to prom and didn't want to hide. We wore matching tuxes, with satin lapels and sequinned cummerbunds. The photos are still in albums at my parents' house.

"We caused quite the stir," I say, "walking into the gym holding hands. We'd been friends for a long time, but I don't think anyone really knew it was more than that."

"Bet you were cute," Tripp says as he tongues my earlobe. "Little teenage bear cub. What was your date like?"

I grin. "Skinny. Boney. He got buff later. I saw a picture of him and his husband on social media. They bicycled across Canada last summer. My God, the thighs on him, they could—"

"Hey!" Tripp pumps harder, making the sleeve squelch in an unsexy way. "None of that. I don't like to share."

"You asked." I pout, but he kisses me, sucking on my lower lip without losing the rhythm below. I twitch, and he smooths a hand over my chest again, shushing me.

"Keep talking."

"Um. So, Eliot and I . . . I didn't realize that going to prom together would be such a big deal. It was like celebrities trying to do their grocery shopping. We just wanted to dance and have fun with our friends and people kept wanting to take our picture or have their picture taken with us, like it was Comic Con or something."

"Oh, you poor baby," Tripp murmurs. I'm breathing hard, and I have to gather my thoughts to remember what comes next.

"After like an hour, Eliot asked if I wanted to leave. I was kind of sad. The sun was barely even down, and I'd gone through so much, told my family, saved the money to buy us both boutonnieres. But he had a car, and he said we'd just go back to his place and have our own party."

Tripp's stills. "OMG, bumblebee, is this the story of how you lost your virginity?"

I wrap my hand around his and push my hips up. "You said you wouldn't stop if I kept talking."

"But is it?" He's sitting up again, blue eyes sparkling.

"Do you want to know or not?" I can come a hell of a lot easier with my hand than this stupid thing.

He bites at a nipple and resumes his stroking, making my eyes roll back in my head. I groan, and my toes curl. "So we went back to his house. His parents were away, and we had the whole place to ourselves."

"Oh, Dougie." My name is almost a growl. Tripp licks his lips. "I really like where this is going."

I flush, in part from arousal, and in part because he can't even guess where this is going, and now I'm worried he's going to think it's dumb.

But I keep talking. "He had this basement home theatre. Big screen that rolled down from the ceiling, surround-sound speakers. And the whole room was specially insulated so you couldn't — Oh, Jesus, Tripp." My hips rock up, thrusting into the slick, tight space.

"Keep talking."

"It was dark, and quiet, and he asked me what I wanted to watch, and I said he could pick." My eyes are closed, and I can picture it all so clearly. The cool leather seeping through my shirt once I'd taken my jacket off. The smell of popcorn that sits in a bowl between us. The—

Tripp slides the masturbator up my cock, pausing just before the tip slips out. I whine, trying to find the angle I need to push back into it, but I need to plant my feet to do it, and I can't find the muscles in my legs to get there. All of me is concentrated on the mere inch of my body currently encased in silicone and lube.

"You stopped talking." Tripp's voice is evil. I hate him and want him so much right now.

"So he picked out a DVD." I sigh as he slides down again. He's working hard now, long pulls that have me aching, before he switches up and jerks me only around the very tip. Half the words coming out of my mouth aren't even words, but he's true to his promise, and if I keep trying, so does he.

"It was—it was—oh God, Tripp, I—"

"You're doing amazing, kitten whiskers. Almost there."

It's weird. I almost feel like I've been tied down, but my limbs are free. I could grab him. Pin him. We have lube and condoms, and I could be inside him in a minute. But I don't want to. This feels so good. I can't remember when sex has ever felt like this. Calvin hasn't made me feel this wanted and this powerful in a long time.

Then why was I with him?

I'm starting to think I don't know.

"Doug?"

I cheat for a second and grab Tripp's hand, holding him still while I push up into the sleeve. God, it feels amazing. I want to thrust into it over and over until I burst, but Tripp is *tsk*ing in my ear, and the muscles in his arms have gone tight and rigid, and I know he let me have that one for free, but he won't let me have another.

I try to find my place in the story again. "So he sat back down next to me. And he took my hand. He said, 'You're going to love this.'" I can still see his smile in the dark. "And it was—it—Tripp!" A tingling is forming in my low back, and the muscles in my thighs jump.

He kisses me, his tongue pushing into my mouth. "This is so much hotter than I thought it would be."

"It was *The Philadelphia Story*. And it was perfect. Stewart and Hepburn. And Grant. Oh my God, Cary Grant. It was the first time I ever—and he—and—" The pressure is unbearable. "He was so handsome and so charming. His jaw and his scowl, like he saw everything." It's the same direct gaze I get from Tripp, and suddenly I can see it so clearly. The same straight nose, the same firm mouth. "He was everything." I can't help myself as both my hands wrap around Tripp and the toy. I push up one more time, and the tight sucking slide pulls me over the edge. My whole body arches off the mattress, and I can't remember ever coming so hard. Tripp grinds against my thigh, and his mouth is sealed over mine, swallowing my shouts, which is good, because even if we're in the last cabana, no one would be able to ignore the noise I'm making if it weren't muffled.

I twitch for a long time after. My throat is dry, and I need a drink, but every time I think about moving, little sparks shoot along my nerve endings, and lying there seems like a better, safer idea.

Tripp's in the little bathroom at the back, running water. Cleaning up the sleeve? I feel like there's no way to get it fully clean again, out here away from sanitizers and hot water.

When he comes back out, I don't even have the sense to put my shorts back on or cover myself with a towel. My body and dick are thoroughly spent, and I can only lie there with glazed eyes.

"Did you know that was going to happen?" I ask.

"That you would tell me about your sexual awakening via Cary Grant and come yourself into a coma?" He shakes his head. "No one could have predicted that." Tripp nudges me until I find it in myself to scoot over, and he presses himself against me, kissing my cheek while his fingers dance little circles in my chest hair. "But it was the hottest fucking thing I've ever seen. You okay?" He nuzzles along my jaw.

"Mm-hmm." I feel like I could sleep for a year.

"Gonna take a nap?"

"Might." I should be considerate. He just got me off in the most astonishing way, and now he's hard too. I should return the favour. But when I fumble for him, his fingers tangle in mine, and he brings them back up to my stomach.

"It's okay, lily pad. We'll get there."

That's nice. I would have tried, but this is better.

As I'm about to drop off, I feel his lips against my temple. I turn towards him, trying to return the gesture, but I'm all heavy and slow and nothing quite works out as I planned.

Nothing has worked out like I planned in the last week, and right now I'm so glad for it.

Just as I go under, I think I hear him say, "Doug, I—" but I slip into sleep before he can finish the rest.

18

TRIPP

*M*y plan has backfired. Lessons learned today:

1—Don't ever assume everything can be fixed with sex toys.

2—Ignoring a wider world with a dipshit fiancé waiting for your fake husband does not protect your feelings in any meaningful way.

3—If you want the kind of orgasm that will make you see white, I *highly* recommend a combination cock ring and butt plug with a silicone strap holding them together. Get the aforementioned fake husband to blow you while he plays with the strap. The movement of the plug on your prostate, not to mention the occasional snap of the strap on your taint, is pretty much guaranteed to melt your brain.

But yeah. I sort of thought, when I packed up my bag of tricks this morning, that I'd distract us with sex, and instead we're both so blissed out we have to be chased out of the cabana by a harried attendant who finds us cuddling in the hammock, and we almost miss the boat. And every second I'm pressed up against Doug, his warm body, crinkly hair, and scent of sun and sweat, I can feel him slipping further under my skin.

The LSD leprechaun grins maniacally as we let ourselves back into the suite.

"It's elegant casual in the dining room tonight," Doug says as he drops his sunglasses onto the bed.

"What does that mean?" I abandoned all those words—office chic, business preppy—when I opened the daycare. My wardrobe is now almost entirely laundry day hangover with a side of hipster.

He pulls out the daily itinerary that comes every morning with breakfast, scanning down the list, brows furrowed. "Here it is. Join us for a night of casual elegance. Collared shirts for the gentlemen, skirts and dresses for the ladies. Didn't you get it in the pre-cruise email?"

For a second, I'm annoyed. Here I am, trying to figure out how I'm going to purge Doug from my senses—how I'm going to forget the way he whimpers in his sleep like a puppy or the tickle of his beard on my balls as he brings me to brain-melting orgasm—and he's worried about a dress code memo?

"I'll figure it out."

"I need a quick shower. Wash the salt water off." He kisses my cheek like I've made him happy, and the annoyed part of me melts, because I'm so screwed when it comes to Doug and my feelings.

I rummage through my suitcase and find one button-down shirt and a pair of slim-fit chinos I threw in just in case we got really unlucky and it rained the whole time we were on vacation, because I'm from Vancouver and we never truly believe it's sunny somewhere else until we get there.

Unfortunately, the shirt is hopelessly wrinkled and the pants aren't much better, so when Doug comes back out of the shower with a towel snug around his waist and a hopeful glint in his eye, I dart around him through the door, my clothes on hangers, and ignore that we totally could have had a pre-dinner quickie, because suddenly I'm worried my pretend—*why did he have to be pretend?*—husband will think I'm a slob if I don't steam the wrinkles out.

I take longer than I should, but the water is barely hot, and I want to give that shirt the best possible chance to relax back into shape. It's mostly better when I step out of the shower into the tiny humid bathroom, and I towel off hurriedly and slide into my clothes, hoping the heat from my body will get them the rest of the way there.

"I hope this is okay," I say as I walk back into the suite, scrubbing my hair with a towel. "I guess if I'd known you before, you would have told me about the memo and—"

Breathing is suddenly optional.

Staring is all I'm capable of doing.

Doug is standing in the middle of the room in a navy blue suit. The shirt underneath is so crisp, it's almost like a second skin, and his tie is a shiny silk two shades darker than his jacket.

He smooths down the front, even though it all fits him perfectly, and the glint of gold on his left hand catches my eye. My own hand goes reflexively to the ring on my finger, the one that isn't mine but has become so comfortable I haven't thought about it in days.

I know what this is.

Shit.

He's wearing his wedding suit, and I'm standing here dressed like the intern who forgot to ask Mom to wash and iron his shirts.

Doug tugs at a cuff. "Is it . . . is it okay?"

I open my mouth to tell him he's perfect, but words require air and my lungs are still on hiatus. Instead, I stumble forwards, bare feet sluggish on the carpet, until I basically collapse into his arms and try to swallow his whole mouth in a clumsy kiss.

He laughs anyway, strong body vibrating against mine. He pulls me close, and I'm so afraid to wrinkle him before I get a chance to look at him again. Admire him. *Mine.* He's mine. He's dressed up for me.

I groan at the brush of his fingers over the front of my pants. Dinner is soon, and my poor cock had quite the adventure this afternoon, but if he wants to, I'll try.

The metallic sound of the zipper is incredibly loud, and my cheeks heat. A few more seconds and I won't be able to stand up.

Then he pats my belly and presses his lips to my ear. "Your fly was down."

I have to put a hand on the dresser as he squeezes past me. "What?"

"Come on. Time for supper!"

I don't remember what I eat that night. All I can picture is the image of Doug unbuttoning his jacket as he sits down. How he smiles at the server as she takes our order and raises his glass to me in a toast as drinks are brought to our table. He's like fucking James Bond—or Carey Grant—and I can't take my eyes off him.

"You look amazing." It might be the first coherent thing I've said since I came out of the shower.

He ducks his head and fiddles with the silver and blue cuff-links at his wrists. "I wanted to—" His mouth screws up for a second. "I wish I'd met you before."

Before? Before when? Before his fiancé ditched him on their wedding day? Before he even met Cowardly Calvin?

Except I can't find the words to speak, because all I can do is catalogue the way Doug's beard has grown out in the last few days, and how it must have been perfectly—maybe profession-ally—trimmed the day of his wedding, and the way his hands are tanned now and how maybe there's a tan line under his wedding band and—*oh God*—what if I have a similar line on my hand too? I've been marked, inside and out. It was all supposed to be fun and pretend, and now it's not and—

So all I say is, "It would have been different, before."

And before he can tell me why I'm wrong or ask me what I mean or why it wouldn't have mattered, they bring our appetizers—Caesar salad for Doug; fuck if I know for me—and I keep my mouth full of food for as long as I possibly can, because the alternative is blurting out the million and one feelings currently stewing inside of me, and it's not fair to Doug to do that. I promised pretend, and my feelings are so very real.

After dinner, we wander around for a while. The idea of going back to the suite makes me anxious, in part because it's practically inevitable we'll have sex again and I won't be able to keep my distance when he's inside me and touching me and saying my name like he does, and in part because going back means today is over and tomorrow is our last day, and I don't know what to do.

Doug's taken off his jacket and is carrying it over one shoulder on a crooked finger. He's rolled up the sleeves of his shirt, so he looks like a rugged male model about to take lunch with someone important. And instead he's strolling through the shopping concourse with his supposed husband who couldn't even iron his shirt.

"There's a late-night comedy act," he says. "Do you want to check it out?"

My Dougster. Always planning ahead. Whether he's suggested it out of genuine interest or because he also knows that going back to the suite carries way too much with it, I'm not sure, so I nod gratefully and say, "Sounds great."

Except we walk into the ship's auditorium, and the lights are already low. We slip into a row about halfway down, apologizing to the people who have to stand to let us by. And, when the lights come up again, instead of the usual things you'd expect for a comedian—a mic stand, a stool, bottle of water—a tall slim man in a plum-coloured suit is standing under the lights in front of heavy drapes. He's the cruise director. I've seen him schmoozing with guests all week.

"Hi, everyone," he says. "I'm really sorry to tell you that tonight's act had to cancel. He was supposed to meet us in Haiti, but unfortunately his plane got stuck in Florida."

A not-insignificant audience is seated in the rows around us, and there's a rustle of questions, but the cruise director holds up a hand. His hair is slick, and his smile is glossy. "I know, I know. I'm disappointed too. But I promise we have something great planned for you. So many of you are here with loved ones. Cruises are so romantic, don't you think?"

My skin crawls, because it's like he's talking right to me, but the people around us laugh and applaud in agreement. The cruise director's grin spreads. "I thought so. And that's why we thought it would be an amazing night to play"—he lifts a hand up behind him and, on cue, the curtains rise, revealing a retro game show set as he proudly proclaims— "It's *The Newlywed Game!*"

. . .

. . .

No.

Fucking.

Way.

I blank out for a second. What are the possible odds? But the crowd is cheering, and even Doug applauds politely. The cruise director is puffing out his chest and strutting across the stage like a true game show host. Maybe this won't be so bad.

"We need some volunteers!" He puts one hand to his brow as he scans the audience. I try to breathe. He'll never pick us. Games like this and ships like this are too heteronormative for him to risk asking the gay guys if they want to play. And even if they do, we can always say no.

A forty-something couple is the first on the stage. They say their names are Bill and Nicole, and they've been married for seventeen years. Then the cruise director picks out a couple older than my grandparents. Their names are Robert and Patricia, and they've been married for fifty-nine years.

"And now I need a couple of true newlyweds. What do you think, everyone, can we find a couple here on their honeymoon?"

I slump lower in my seat. He won't pick us. He won't even look at us. He'll see two brothers on vacation, and his eyes will skip right over us.

"Here!" a voice says next to me. "Here! They're on their honeymoon!"

The ensuing sequence of events is a slow-motion nightmare. I turn my head, and the first thing I see is the finger pointed in my face. I blink, and the finger drops. Someone has turned a spotlight in our direction, illuminating the woman next to me, and all I feel is horror.

Myrna is sitting beside me. I haven't seen her since that first day in the hot tub, but she looks utterly pleased with herself.

"They're newlyweds!" she says again. Her smile in my direction is pure delight.

Motherfucking Matchmaking Myrna.

19

DOUG

I don't have to make speeches very much at my job. Programming directors mostly sit in dark rooms watching movies and emailing lists back and forth to their staff and the festival director. Sometimes I have to introduce someone else at a fundraiser.

Walking onto a stage under a spotlight while people cheer is not my idea of a good time. Not even Tripp's hand in mine makes the experience comfortable. But the people clapping and urging us on while we stared at each other in the audience was not any better, so eventually I pulled Tripp to his feet and pushed him past meddling Myrna.

"Hello! Hello. And who are you?" The cruise director's eyes dance as he shakes both our hands.

Tripp and I glance at each other. I telepathically tell him what a terrible idea this is, and I'm pretty sure that's regret flashing in his eyes.

"My name's Tripp," he says. "And this is my husband, Doug."

My heart squeezes when he says it. How many more times will I get to be his husband?

"Great!" The director says it like we're the most interesting people in the world. "And where are you from, Tripp and Doug?"

He holds the microphone in front of me, so it must be my turn to answer. "Um. Toronto, Canada."

"Canadians! So polite. And how long have you been married?"

Tripp and I glance at each other again before he leans into the mic and says, "A week."

What a week.

"Amazing! Why don't you join the other contestants?"

We settle on a too-firm leather love seat. Tripp drops his arm around my shoulder, and I put one hand on his knee, mostly to ground myself. The host is talking, explaining how the game works, and people in the audience are laughing, and I can't really hear any of it because my pulse is roaring in my ears like a laundry machine.

"You okay?" Tripp asks. "If you want to run off the stage and go back to the room, I'll be right behind you."

My hand tightens, and his free hand slides over mine. Our two rings lay on top of each other, and the sight of them together draws out a long exhale from my lungs. I give Tripp a wobbly smile. "I'll be fine." We'll never see these people again, and I am not ready to stop being Tripp's husband, no matter how uncomfortable the situation.

He presses his lips to my temple. I feel like I should be shy, with an auditorium of strangers watching, but we look like exactly what they think we are: two gay men hopelessly in love.

Shit. That's not what I mean. We're not—we're—

"Who will go first?"

I don't realize right away the cruise director's question is directed at us. I must look like the picture of horror when I turn to Tripp, because he kisses me again—chastely so as not to upset the grannies in the house—and says, "I'll handle it."

I'm escorted off the stage, along with Nicole and Patricia.

We're led to a small set of chairs, and Patricia sits next to me. Her white hair is a swirling nest around her head, set off by star-burst earrings that she's probably owned for almost as long as she's been married.

"What's your husband's name?" she asks.

"Tripp." I sit up straighter when I don't hesitate on the answer.

She pats my hand. "He's very handsome."

I can't help my smile. "He really is." Then I lean in closer. "Do you know how this game works?"

Her whole face lights up in a twinkling smile that rivals her earrings. "Honey, I was watching *The Newlywed Game* before your parents were out of high school."

It feels like we sit backstage a long time, but then just as suddenly, a staff person is ushering us back on stage. The audience applauds, and my eyes seek out Tripp. Someone has brought out tall stools and set one behind each of the love seats. Tripp is sitting on the one farthest from the cruise director, and he gives me a reassuring smile as I take the seat in front of him.

He leans forwards, strong hands massaging my shoulders. "We got this, buttercup. Just like trivia night."

I sit up a bit straighter. Trivia night? He shouldn't have said that. I'm not a particularly competitive person. Sports aren't my thing, and even in school, I was always a middling student at best. But I'm weirdly competitive about things like trivia and board games. And he's just lumped this in with those, so now we have to win.

I glance down the row where the two women have rejoined their husbands. Tripp's thumbs dig into the tendons at the back of my neck.

"They're going down," I mutter, and he kisses the hinge of my jaw.

"Now, now," the cruise director says, swaggering towards us. "No giving away the answers."

I reach behind me to pat Tripp's hand. We're not going to win by cheating. We're better than that.

"All right! Let's start with our newlyweds!" The director says, and I'm handed a small whiteboard and a marker. "Doug. Can I call you Doug?"

"I, uh—" I shift to one side as he sits down, mic held in my direction. "Yes,"

"All right. And you and Tripp are on your honeymoon? He says you had a bit of a whirlwind romance."

I nod, ignoring the urge to glance back at Tripp. Whirlwind indeed.

"So the first question should be an easy one for you, because it's about the first time you met."

"I remember it clearly," I say into the mic.

"Mm-hmm. We want to see how well you remember it. What was Tripp wearing, the first time you met?"

I freeze. Oh no. I can't tell them. I— How can I possibly explain that—

His bathing suit? Is that what I should write down? Maybe we met at the pool? He swims laps and I—

A sound stops me just as the marker touches the whiteboard. I glance up, and the sound comes again. In the front row, two boys who can't be more than seventeen are giggling. When they catch me looking at them, they slump down in their seats, smothering laughs behind their hands.

Tripp's pretty shameless. What if he told the truth? No way teenage boys are giggling about me meeting my husband at the pool.

Behind me, Tripp clears his throat softly.

Here we go.

I set the marker down and turn the blank whiteboard around to face the audience.

"What—what did—" The director's smooth demeanor cracks. "You didn't write anything."

The corners of my mouth are twitching, and if I'm wrong, I hope Tripp will forgive me for exposing this secret. "Yes, I wrote nothing. Because that's what Tripp was wearing the first time we met."

The audience bursts into laughter and applause. The cruise director is beaming like Stanley Tucci in *The Hunger Games*. "Tripp, what did you say?"

I turn, and Tripp is holding his own whiteboard. On it, a single word is written: *nothing.*

Some of the tension along my spine relaxes.

The next question is about Tripp's worst habit around the house. I have no way of knowing this. I say he leaves his underwear lying around. Apparently he said he never washes the dishes. We'll have to talk about that. Nothing grosses me out quite like yesterday's milk at the bottom of the cereal bowl.

"And the last question is, it's Sunday morning. You wake up to find Tripp isn't home. Where is he?"

The question does the opposite of what's intended. Instead of one specific answer, it floods my brain with a million images of waking up in bed with Tripp, like we did this morning. He's sleepy and rumpled, and he smiles at me while he calls me "lemon bar" or something equally silly before he wanders off naked to go make the coffee.

I want so many mornings just like that one.

"Doug?" the director prompts.

I blink, scattering the fantasy. "Sorry." I take a deep breath and try again. Okay. Let's say it's real. We're living together, maybe we get a cute apartment close to the lake. It's Sunday morning. We have nowhere to be. Tripp's not going to work on a Sunday. Or is he? He's moved the doggie daycare to Toronto, and dogs have to be walked, right? Except it's daycare, so the dogs are all home for the weekend and—

"Oh." The answer is obvious. The dogs have all gone home

for the weekend. "He's walking Trixie," I say, scribbling on the whiteboard.

The director smiles, leaning in closer. "And who is Trixie?"

Why is this the question that brings tears to my eyes? Softly, I say, "She's our dog."

I've never had a dog, but now I want one like I want my next breath. I want Tripp and Trixie and a cozy little life where we take her out in the mornings and drink coffee at our favourite café or let her run down the beach while the waves roll in.

The people are clapping and the director rises from his spot next to me, moving on to the next couple. Tripp is still somewhere behind me, and I can't make myself turn around, because if I do, I'll tell him all of it right now, here on this stage, surrounded by strangers who think we're married and who will be so confused when I drop to my knees and tell him he can't go back to Vancouver. That I want everything I've just imagined. Him and me, a place of our own. I want to meet Trixie, and I will bribe her with every kind of treat and squeaky toy until she decides she loves me, and then we will be our own little eight-legged family.

I want that more than I've ever wanted anything, because I want Tripp. And the realization sparks something like panic in my chest, because how can it be possible? I met him six days ago. I was with Calvin for three years. And yet I never wanted him the way I do Tripp.

In the end, we don't win *The Newlywed Game*. Robert and Patricia bring the house down in the second round when one of the questions is about the most memorable time they ever had sex, and they both tell an identical story about a romp in an Istanbul hot tub in 1977.

The cruise director thanks us for playing along and hands us our consolation prize—another deck of branded playing cards —but I'm not disappointed. Because I'm going home with Tripp. Back to the honeymoon suite that is ours and—I hope—will be the site of some of our most memorable sex when we're asked the question fifty years from now.

"My best friend's name is Pierce," Tripp says, as we wait for the elevator.

"Hmm?" I say, too busy planning lazy mornings in bed and brunches on sunny patios.

"The question about who was the first person I called after we got engaged?"

"Oh." That had been one of the questions they asked me first in the second round. I think I said he called his parents. At least that question had been suitably PG and I hadn't had to tell everyone about the cabana and the cock ring and the noises Tripp made as he came down my throat.

His hand slides into mine. "I would have called Pierce. I'd want him to be my best man."

Makes sense. "My sister Kate was going to be my maid of honour."

The elevator doors slide open, and we step inside and Tripp says, "Oh, sweetheart. I didn't mean to—" And I realize he thinks he's upset me. Because every other time I've mentioned the wedding-that-wasn't, the conversation dies and we have to wait for me to pull myself together. But it's not like that anymore. It's almost like those horrible fifteen minutes happened to another person. A much sadder person. Someone who was shuffling through life and would have wound up married to someone I'm not even really sure I know anymore.

"No," I say, making sure I'm smiling. We're the only two people in the elevator, so I press right into him. "No, it's okay. I'm okay. We can talk about it, but there really isn't anything to say. I think I'm over it."

He arches an eyebrow, but his hands are on my hips. "You are?"

I kiss him, trying to tell him everything I've realized, everything I know. His grip on me tightens.

"Tripp, I'm okay," I say again. "I'm fine. Getting married was going to be a mistake, and I know that now."

"You do?"

I brush his nose with mine. "I do. Because then I never would have met you. Tripp, I think I love you."

20

TRIPP

No time for lists, because he loves me.

He spends all night telling me over and over with his words and his body. He is strong and confident as he talks to me about the life he imagines for us in Toronto, while his fingers brush over my ribs and across my thighs. He holds my body open for him to claim, even while his words crack open my heart in a way I don't think will ever heal.

This sweet man, who I only ever want to make smile, loves me.

And I am so fucking scared.

Usually I'm the one who falls hard and fast. Never before have I been the one to put the brakes on.

But as he tells me about how much Trixie will like walking on the beach near his house and how much he needs me, all I can think is this is some kind of fever dream that he's going to wake up from and realize he's put too much hope in someone who is a serial dater with a track record of short but intense relationships.

Doug is the marrying kind. I am the *let's pretend we're married for shits and giggles* kind. The distance between us is huge and I think—*no, I know*—he doesn't see it.

I sleep so poorly, while Doug is wrapped around me like a snuggly furry blanket, that at two in the morning, I go down to the business center.

Dear P,

I screwed up and I don't know how to fix this.

T

Anything I say is going to smash poor Doug's heart into tiny bloody pieces. And it's not that I don't want him. Not that I don't love him too. But he's got stars in his eyes—stars I know too well, along with that special kind of shame that comes when you realize the object of your admiration will never live up to the fantasy you created—and if there's one thing that makes me more afraid than the idea Doug might be right and we could be something amazing, it's that he'll eventually realize I'm not who he thought I was and regret everything we've had.

I'm on the balcony as the sun comes up. It's our last full day at sea, and I'd love for the twisting feeling in my stomach to be seasickness, but it's dread that the next step is all mine to make.

My grip on the railing tightens at the sound of the balcony door sliding open. Strong hands slide around me, and Doug's beard makes me shiver before he plants a kiss on my neck.

"Morning."

I twist my head so his kisses reach my cheek. "Morning."

"Trouble sleeping?"

"No." My voice is rough, but I let him think it's from the number of times I screamed his name last night and not some other emotion. "Just wanted to see the sunrise."

His kisses keep going, while his hands start to roam over my body. Despite everything I'm feeling, I can't help responding, because his touch is so earnest and his body is so much the perfect shape and size for all my fantasies that I'm helpless when he decides he wants me.

He undoes the tie of my robe and growls when he discovers I'm not wearing anything underneath. It's oddly reminiscent of the first time we met, except here he's helping me take my clothes off.

And he wasn't naked last time.

The robe hits the ground, and he kicks it behind us. He's hard and slides his cock against my ass, and I groan.

"Sore?" he asks.

I am, but not so much that I'm going to turn him down. I reach around to hold his head close while I push back against his erection. Whatever misgivings I might have, we're still on the ship and our week isn't up. He wants me and I want him, and it can still be that simple.

We're on our honeymoon, after all.

He's come prepared; lube and condoms appear at hand without any fuss. Since this is an encore performance after last night, it takes hardly any time for him to work me open with his fingers, but I'm still shaking and begging as he does it.

"Doug. Doug, please. Fuck me. Please."

His cock is thick and heavy and delicious as he pushes into me. A shudder ripples over me, from my toes to the roots of my hair, while his hot breath brushes over my skin.

"You think anyone is awake yet?" he asks, and I'd been so caught up in the sensation of him that I'd forgotten we have neighbors. Close ones. They may not be able to see us, but they'll *hear* me if I'm not careful.

Except then he thrusts in hard, so he's seated all the way in my ass, and the only thing that stops me from shouting is his hand over my mouth.

"Fuck," I whisper when I can breathe again. I'm braced on the balcony, and his hands come around to grip the rail on either side of mine. He's pumping into me, breathing fast, and every thrust is taking up more room in my body and wiping away my concerns. We can do this. He's strong and fierce. We can do this together.

"Tripp." His beard scrapes over my shoulder, making me whine.

"Yes. Yes, please."

"I love you."

Somewhere far away, I remember I'm supposed to be afraid, but the friction of our bodies together, the heat and earnestness of his words, are condensing my whole existence into a tight ball of need in my gut, and nothing else matters.

He shifts, letting go of the rail so he can dig his fingers into my hip bones, pulling me tight against him. His dick presses hard against my prostate, making my knees go wobbly, but he's so big, so strong, and his palm spreads over my stomach while his other hand starts to pump my cock. I'd scream if I could, but since we're still trying not to scandalize any early risers, I tilt my head back and pant.

He comes with a grunt, teeth on my shoulder, but he keeps working me, grip tight and insistent until I follow him over the edge, spurting all over the glass in front of me.

"Oh. Oh my God." My whole body is heaving. The space between us is slick with sweat. He needs to get out of my ass and deal with the condom, but I wrap myself around him like a backwards pretzel, because if we stay like this forever, I won't ever need to worry again.

"I've never felt this way with anyone," he says, and all I can do is nod, because neither have I. So hopelessly in love and simultaneously so responsible for another person's happiness.

It's an uncomfortable fit.

The *bong bong* sounds and, just like that, the spell is broken. Doug gives my ass a squeeze and disappears into the shower. I manage to get my robe back on in time to open the door when breakfast arrives and then take my turn in the bathroom. My body is a minefield of hickeys and finger marks, and I trace every one of them, because they're from Doug, and regardless of what happens when we get back to Canada, I will always treasure anything he gives me.

The pool decks are crowded, but we find two loungers on the upper level near the walking track. Doug chatters happily all day. It's like realizing he's in love is the tsunami that wipes out all the dams holding him back before. He tells me about his mom and his sisters while we have lunch at the buffet. He talks about the film festival, and all the movies he's looking forward to this year. Doug really is a basketball fan. The Raptors have won a championship, and he grumbles about how they still don't get the respect they deserve. I would not have pictured shy, sad Doug as a rowdy sports fan, but this one, this happy, bubbly, incarnation, I can totally see screaming his head off from the stands.

The wedding really did a number on his self-confidence. His dad's death too. I'm sorry he's struggled so much.

This new Doug is charming. But the change drives home how much I don't know about him.

And clearly he doesn't know that I'm a fucking coward, but I do, especially when I choose the easy out and trash talk about how the NBA Eastern Conference will always be a bridesmaid to the Western Conference.

Dinner is a blur. I couldn't tell you what I ate. Doug, of course, has the Caesar salad but goes out on a limb and orders the pork loin. His face scrunches up as he takes the first bite, but then he looks at me and says, "It tastes like chicken."

We go back to the suite, and I'm so wound up I can't sit still, but also the space seems so small that I feel like I have nowhere to go. I end up back on the balcony, taking long slow breaths, when I hear the door behind me again.

He stands beside me, shoulder to shoulder, pinkie finger rubbing against mine.

"You okay?" he asks.

"Yeah," I say, forcing as much enthusiasm as I can into it. The night is dark, and the only light is what spills out from the room behind us, so his face is mostly in shadow, and that means—thankfully—mine must be too.

He stares up at the sky. I memorize every line of his profile.

He says, "I'm not naive, you know."

My heart stops. "What?"

Doug's gaze drops to me, and his smile is soft. "I know you can't plan a life with someone after only one week. It's impossible to know them well enough to be confident they're your future. But, Tripp—" He takes my hand. "I don't want this to be the end. We live across the country from one another. I know a cruise ship isn't real life. But I want this. Us. I want to get to know you in the real world. I want to fight with you about leaving your dishes on the counter and whose turn it is to walk the dog. You've done so much for me this week, made me feel stronger than I have in years. We'll be so good together. Don't you feel that?"

I do. Oh my God, I do, but I've felt it before, and every time I was wrong, and loving Doug is—there's so much at stake.

"What are you asking?" My voice shakes.

"I'm asking you to try. With me. I don't know how we'll make the geography work. But I care about you too much to let that be the reason we don't try."

I want to laugh and cry at the same time. Does he think time zones are the biggest hurdle we have to get over?

"Please." He kisses me, confident, brave, and I want to sink into it and let it carry me away.

I don't want this to be over either. And maybe the distance will be good. I can't get in over my head with four thousand kilometres between us. We'll have to take it slow, unless we want to rack up a ton of debt to see each other. Maybe it will be enough to protect us until we know for sure.

"Okay," I say, and his lips curve into a smile against mine.

"Yeah?"

I am a selfish, weak fool, but how can I say no to this man who loves me when I love him too?

We talk late into the night. Doug tells me more about Toronto. I tell him about all the places Trixie and I like to go on walks, and the Thai place Pierce discovered that makes the best basil pork I have ever had. As it gets later, our conversation dissolves into nonsensical tangents. Stories about childhood and families and terrible first dates. It's like we're trying to tell each other everything, so that if we never see each other again, we'll already know everything there is to know.

I don't remember falling asleep, but when I wake, it's daylight, and Doug's head is on my chest.

The ship is oddly silent. Not that it was ever really noisy before. The sound of the engine has never been louder than an average residential air conditioner, but now that the engine has stopped, the room is eerily quiet.

I lift my head. In the distance, I can see the condo towers of Miami Beach.

I lie back down, pulling Doug to me, inhaling his scent and trying to memorize the texture of his hair and the weight of him as he sleeps on my body.

But eventually the morning announcements sound, letting us know about very official things like "disembarkation procedures" and Doug stirs and rubs sleep from his eyes while he scratches the hairy belly that I will never get enough of.

"Good morning," he says softly, and his gentle smile seals it for me. Despite everything, despite all my past history that says this feeling never lasts, I want to see that smile again, on so many different mornings.

"Hi."

"Are we here?"

I press my lips against his temple. "Mm-hmm."

He presses a thigh between my legs. "Is there time before we have to leave?"

"You're insatiable."

"The festival is in three months. I can't get out to see you until after that. I'm stocking up." We have each other's phone numbers, but phone calls are going to be a poor substitute when I'm missing everything about him.

The good news is there's no room service breakfast on the last morning, so we have the place to ourselves.

Disembarkation is tedious and slow. It involves a lot of time spent sitting in the dining lounge waiting for our number to be called. I text Pierce to let him know we're back in the lower forty-eight and to confirm he'll pick me up in Vancouver when I land. My flight back is a disaster of layovers and connections, and since I don't live at Liam's anymore, I'm back to crashing in Pierce's guest room. The last thing I want is to struggle with cabs or transit when I get home.

We collect our suitcases from a conveyor belt in the cruise port. Happy staff members thank us for coming and point us towards the exit. Outside, it's a bright, humid day, and the line for taxis is a mile long, with porters running back and forth.

I need a second before the unexpectedly familiar face in the crowd catches my attention. He's wearing a tropical shirt and Ray Bans, and he's obscured for a minute by a guy carrying a huge bouquet of flowers. But then I spot the white-blond hair again, and I can't help myself when I drop Doug's hand and break into a run.

"Pierce?"

He's scanning the crowd, but when he hears his name, his gaze locks on mine, and he breaks into a grin.

"Hey!"

"What are you doing here?" I wrap him up in a big bear hug, laughing.

"I got called down on a last-minute audit. This new flight tech company they're thinking about buying at work." Pierce is an in-house lawyer for a private equity firm. They send him all over the place to talk to companies they're considering investing in. "Finished up yesterday, and I knew you'd be back this morning, so I added an overnight at the hotel." He lifts his sunglasses and drops his voice. "And your last email sounded like you could use a friend."

I gape, scrambling to remember what I'd said in the email, then shuffling the pieces around until the last twenty-four hours make up part of the puzzle too. "No. No, it's fine. I mean, it's great to see you, but I'm fine. More than fine."

"Really?" He doesn't look convinced, but then he's been the recipient of far too many of my tears and diatribes when my past relationships fail.

"Uh-huh. In fact, there's someone I want you to meet. Doug! Hey!" I turn, but Doug's not at my shoulder the way I thought he was. I whirl, and he's not anywhere. "Doug?"

I spot him maybe twenty feet away. His eyebrows are scrunched together, and his jaw is tight as he speaks to someone. Something's not right, and I hurry towards him.

"Doug? Hey. What's going on?"

His eyes widen, and with every step, a quicksand feeling grabs hold of me. His face goes deeper into distress as I approach.

And then I see the man with the flowers.

The man who has a hold of Doug's hand and is speaking quickly to him. He glances nervously between us. He's older than Doug but still handsome. His skin is smooth, his hair neatly trimmed. I can imagine him in a well-tailored suit schmoozing a room full of donors.

I don't need an introduction, but how am I supposed to stop Doug when he opens his mouth to speak?

His words pull me under.

"Tripp. This is Calvin."

21

DOUG

We walk out of the cruise terminal and, for a minute, everything seems too bright. Sunlight reflects off white concrete and people bustle in every direction, looking for buses and shuttles, hailing cabs. I scan the signposts trying to find some identifier for the limo I arranged back when I booked everything. A limo seemed special. Romantic. A nice way to cap off our honeymoon. Of course, I expected Calvin to be riding with me, not Tripp, but as it stands now, that detail is irrelevant because I can't find where we're supposed to be picked up. At this rate, we'll be walking to the airport.

"They said to look for post number five," I say, as a porter nearly runs over my toes with a towering cart of luggage. In the press, I lose Tripp's hand, but I don't have time to worry about it, because suddenly the din gets quiet, the chaos recedes, and I see his face.

Calvin.

He's staring at me, standing stock-still as people swirl around him like he's as permanent a fixture as the lampposts.

He's in a coral-coloured shirt and striped shorts. He looks like hell. Like he hasn't slept the whole time I've been away. Once, I would have been glad to see him looking even half as upset as I did when I first stepped on the plane to Florida, but now all I feel is cold dread despite the hot Miami sun overhead. It roots me to the spot, so I can't do anything but stare as he rushes to me, thrusting a bouquet of dark-red roses at me. They're surprisingly heavy.

"I'm sorry. I'm so sorry." His words are a whispered rush, and I'm still so astonished to see him I barely understand what he's saying. "Doug, I've been thinking about you all week."

Clarity re-emerges. Tripp. Where is Tripp? My head swivels, desperately looking for him. He was there a second ago, but just like Calvin has materialized out of thin air, Tripp has vanished.

"What?" Calvin asks. "What's wrong?"

"What are you doing here?" I sound drunk, maybe drugged, like I'm about to have dental surgery, and I'm pretty sure the next few minutes are going to be about as fun.

"I came—" His eyes are desperate, something I have never seen before from him. He is always the confident one. The one in charge. I let him be the one in charge. Now, though, he says, "Oh God, Doug. I screwed up." He reaches for my hand. My wedding band shines in the sun, and I glance at his naked left hand. Wrong. This is all wrong.

That's when I finally spot Tripp.

He's walking towards us, head cocked to one side, like he knows something is up. Of course he does. He knows me. It's all been so fast, but he knows. We were going to—we were—

I'm going to cry. As he reaches us, tears swell at the edges of my eyes, ready to spill over.

Say something. Anything. My arms tremble under the weight of Calvin's roses.

"Tripp, this is Calvin. Calvin—" It's like I've become a robot, reciting lines that have been fed to me from a central computer. "This is Tripp. He is my . . . " Husband. Husband. In every way that matters. "Friend. I met him on the cruise."

Tripp watches me wordlessly. I want to drop my eyes, embarrassed, like I've done something wrong. But I can't look away. There's a ticking clock in my head, and it says our time together is being measured in minutes, maybe seconds now, and I can't—I can't—

"It's nice to meet you." Tripp shakes Calvin's hand politely. "I've heard a lot."

Calvin gives him a sheepish smile. "Good things I hope."

Tripp wipes his palm on the front of his shirt. "Not really." His eyes swing to mine. "You okay?"

I glance at Calvin, who is waiting with a mix of concern and confusion. He looks so worried, and I wonder how this is the same person who thought he could never mind me a week ago.

Tripp is so close I can practically see his heart pounding just beneath his throat. Or maybe it's only that I can feel my own pulse thundering in my ears.

I drop my gaze to the concrete. "Not okay. Not really."

He wraps my fingers in his. My wedding band pinches my skin at the base of my knuckle, and I wince.

He asks, "What do you need me to do?"

I'm trembling. The air is coming out of my lungs too fast. I'm going to start crying right here in front of all these people trying to get to the airport.

"What's going on?" a man with white-blond hair asks behind Tripp.

"Doug?" Calvin asks. He puts a hand on my arm, and I jerk away from it, closer to Tripp.

"Hey." Tripp's holding on to my shoulders and holding me up in the process. "Hey, cinnamon bun. It's okay. What do you need?"

"Cinnamon bun?" Calvin asks. "Sweetie, who is this guy?"

I shake my head while the world spins around me like those Mexican rain dancers spiralling off their pole. Tripp and Calvin. They can't both be here. It's like a time travel movie where, if you run into your past self, you both stop existing. I'm going to poof out of this plane at any second, and I'll be so sad to never see—

"I—" Words are hard to find. Tripp dips his chin down, trying to meet my gaze.

"It's okay. Whatever you need, I'll do it."

"Doug. I'm sorry. I know it's a surprise to see me here," Calvin says. "But I didn't want you to have to fly home alone. I don't want you to be alone again."

I'm not alone. I'm with Tripp.

"Doug." Tripp's voice is steady. "What do you need?" His eyes are steady too. I can see it. The strength. I felt strong with him. I need to be strong now. We've talked about this. Maybe not quite like this, but we had a plan, and that plan involved me going home and sorting things out with Calvin. Tripp knows that. It's the right thing to do.

But I don't want to. Faced with it all in this moment, the right thing hurts so much.

I take a deep breath, steeling myself for what I have to say. For what we both know I have to say. "I need—I need to talk to him. To hear him out."

Tripp's throat bobs as he swallows. He knows, but the acceptance washing over his sharp features is painful to see.

He squeezes my shaking hand. "Yeah. That's for the best. I get it."

I shake my head slowly, suddenly afraid to look anywhere but at my shoes. Because Tripp is backing away from me, and Calvin is looming behind me like a bogeyman, and I'm the one making this choice.

Tripp steps back until he's shoulder to shoulder with the man with the white-blond hair. "This is my best friend, Pierce Chilton-Barnes-Smith."

I can't tell if that's a joke. One last poke at our Freeman-Gillingham adventures. It hurts too much to ask, so instead I shake Pierce's hand. Maybe I look at his face. I think I'm having an out-of-body experience. People are talking, my body is moving, maybe I'm even saying things, but I'm not in control of any of it.

"Those are quite the flowers," Pierce says.

"Oh," Calvin says sheepishly. "Yeah. I think there are going to be a lot of apology flowers in my future." The cellophane crinkles as I shrink back, and I'm tempted to throw the whole bouquet on the ground.

"Oh yeah? Sounds like there's a story there." Pierce laughs uncomfortably, and I wonder how much he knows.

"I'll tell you about it in the cab," Tripp says, and my heart ratchets up in my chest, because he's leaving. No. Not yet. Not yet. But what are we going to do? Take a cab together? Sit at the airport bar making small talk while we wait for our flights to be called like we're all friends just back from vacation?

"Where are you headed?" Calvin asks Pierce.

"Vancouver. My company has a jet at an airfield not far from here."

What? Somehow the airport bar plan is appealing now. He's not even coming to the airport. He's going somewhere else. Away from me.

Calvin whistles. "Oh yeah, who do you work for?"

They're chatting, and nausea settles in my stomach. Tripp's hand slides over the small of my back, to that place that grounds me and tells me I'll be okay if I'm with him.

"Hey," he says softly while Calvin and Pierce compare professional notes. "Just say the word and we'll run back on the boat. Float away and seek asylum in Cuba."

My laugh is a wet thing that tries to choke me as I inhale. "Tripp."

He leans in closer. "I really want to kiss you right now."

I shoot a glance at Calvin. He's talking with Pierce, but he's watching me. He'll see if I kiss Tripp.

But what if I never kiss Tripp again?

"No," he says, like he can read my mind. "No. This isn't the end. You do what you have to do, and then you call me or come find me. Send up a pigeon or a flare. All right?"

I nod.

"Doug." He says my name so firmly I have to look at him, and his face wrecks me. His eyes are shining with love, dark blue set a little too deep in his tanned face. "This isn't the end of us, okay?"

I wish I could believe him. I wish we'd had one more day. One more hour. I didn't realize reality would literally be waiting for me outside the door the second we stepped off the ship.

He's pulling at his finger, and I realize with horror he's trying to take off the titanium ring.

"No." I don't even think about it before the word is out of my mouth.

Tripp freezes. "Doug." The shine in his eyes has changed, like he's fighting tears now too.

"It's yours," I say. I don't know why. What if Calvin asks about it? What's Tripp even going to do with it? Wear it when he gets back to Vancouver and explain that no, he's not married, and yes, the ring actually belongs to someone else, but no, he didn't steal it, it was a gift from a man who isn't his husband?

"We need to get going if we want to catch our flight," Calvin says. I want to push him in front of one of the buses as they pull away from the curb.

"Sure," Tripp says again. This is it. Time to go with him or time to leave. Time to say something. Anything. But I'm silent, because I'm doing the right thing. So he says, "Send up a flare," and all I can do is nod, words and tears and anger clogging in my throat. Unthinking, I shove the flowers at Pierce, who I still don't know if I've ever said two words to.

Calvin says, "Doug," but fuck him and his roses. I give Tripp one more look, promising myself this won't be the last time, and

I turn, pulling my suitcase and letting Calvin follow if he
wants to.

22

TRIPP

*T*his sucks.

Which part?

All of it, but here's the short list:

1) Somewhere between the cruise terminal and Pierce's plane, I put my sunglasses down, and I can't find them.

2) I'm on a frigging private jet, and I'm not even enjoying myself.

3) Because the thing that sucks the most is that I'm on a private plane without Doug. The last time I wore those sunglasses was with Doug, and now I have neither.

Maybe he still has them, just like I still have the ring on my finger.

"Champagne?" Pierce holds up a bottle from the bar, and all I can think about is the bottle in Doug's suite—our suite—that first day when I was naked. It was there for him and Calvin.

In the end, Calvin got everything.

I tried to be brave, because Doug needed that. I said all the right things. The things we talked about, and the things I knew he needed to hear. I told him that moment wouldn't be our last one.

But now, as we're thousands of feet somewhere over America, I'm struggling to hold on to that conviction.

Calvin surprised me. A guy who couldn't even show up to his wedding isn't someone I would expect to make big romantic gestures. A polite email, yes. Maybe he tries to meet Doug at the airport in Toronto. But coming all the way to Florida and navigating the thousands of people all getting off their ships at the same time just to make sure he found Doug...

My game plan didn't include that, and now I'm second-guessing everything I said and did in those few awful minutes before Doug walked away from me with wobbling steps.

"Do you need to fake a medical emergency and force us to land early?" Pierce asks.

"What?"

He gives me a cocky smile. "Well, I can't ask the pilot to change the flight plan. Waste of company resources and all that. But if you need to go to Toronto, you could fake appendicitis and I could get her to land. I think we're somewhere over Nebraska. They have airports in Nebraska, right?"

I bury my face in my hands. Fake appendicitis is something I would do. Just like I would have tried to charm Doug right there in the parking lot and convince him to stomp on Calvin's toes and run away with me.

But what I want with him doesn't work like that. He needs to go home. Needs to close the chapter of his life with Calvin before we can write one together.

I trust him. I trust that he loves me.

But the farther away we get, the more I worry that I'm not going to be enough to make him come find me on the other side of the country. Life isn't a cruise, and no number of nights playing *The Newlywed Game* is going to prepare us for reality. Calvin proved that today.

Time differences are a bitch, and we're three hours behind Florida time when we land in Vancouver, which only makes the entire surreal day last longer. We go back to Pierce's and order takeout, and Pierce catches me up on gossip among our social circle and reminds me that he truly is the best friend in the world by the way he asks me absolutely nothing else about Doug.

But I nearly choke on a wonton when he asks, "What do you want to do about Liam?"

"What about him?" I wash down the fragments of pork and fried dough with cold beer. With everything else going on, I haven't thought about my ex-boyfriend in days. Why would I?

"Well, all your stuff is still at his place."

Oh. Yeah.

I poke a chopstick in his direction. "I like you ten percent less right now."

———

Liam's in Thailand, as it turns out. I text him to ask about going over to collect my things, and his reply comes in the middle of the night. I have the absurd thought that if he really cared about me, he'd have shown up at the airport, but I know that's just my anxiety and my hurt about Doug and the stunt that Calvin pulled talking. If Liam had turned up with two dozen roses and a heartfelt apology, I'd have pushed him off the pier.

Fortunately, I still have a key to our—his—town house. Packing up my stuff takes less time that I would have thought, and I am a champion packer. I've moved so many times, chasing one guy after another, that when Pierce and I go get boxes, I know exactly how many to buy, down to the square inch.

Most of my things are clothes. Books from an academic life I abandoned. Baskets of dog toys. I take the blue stoneware mugs from the cupboard, because even though Liam and I bought them together, he's never liked them. His life moves too quickly to drink coffee sedately at home. Faster to stand in line with the rest of the hustlers at Starbucks and drink on the go.

This is what my life amounts to. Clothes, books, dog toys, and four coffee cups.

I am not the person you follow across the country.

"Do you need to call him?" Pierce asks.

"No. We don't have anything else to say to each other. He can find the key when he gets back from Thailand." I toss that same key through the letter slot in the front door after I lock up.

Pierce says, "I wasn't talking about Liam."

Oh.

"No."

Doug will call me when he's ready. It's been a day. Calling him now is too soon.

But that doesn't mean I don't spend hours with my phone in my hand that night. Just in case he's already ready.

I tell myself he will call. I wonder what I'll do if he doesn't. Then I tell myself to shut the hell up, because he's going to call. Send a message by pigeon. Something. We promised.

———

Monday brings work, and work brings distraction. My staff—all two of them, Ava and Cherise—have been minding the daycare while I've been away. Cherise has also been taking care of Trixie, and I've never been so glad to see another living creature in my life.

Trixie, that is.

I mean, Cherise is cool and all, but she's also twenty-one, still lives with her parents, and frequently talks about going back to school to become a dental hygienist, so I don't think it would be fair to hang my emotional well-being on her.

Trixie, though, is fair game. She runs up to me when I walk

into the daycare. She's a fluffy, wiggly tornado, and I scoop her up.

"Hey, pretty girl," I say, as she licks my nose. "I know someone who can't wait to meet you. His name is Doug."

I shouldn't have said that. But the second I see her, all I can think about is Doug and *The Newlywed Game* and the feverish way he'd kissed me—sort of like how Trixie is kissing me now, like she's making up for a week of missed opportunities—while he'd told me about his vision for us and our mornings walking Trixie.

I'd be lying if I didn't admit her fur is a little tear-stained by the time I put Trixie down again. Let Cherise and Ava think I just really missed my dog.

They ask about my trip, as do many of our customers as they drop their dogs off for the day. And every single one, all I say is, "Great. So relaxing." Because what else am I going to say? I met a guy, convinced him to pretend to be my husband, and then he went home and I miss him so bad my teeth hurt?

"You don't look relaxed," Ava says. She's in her fifties, divorced twice, and her daughter and three grandkids live with her. She says she works at the daycare because chasing after dogs all day is relaxing compared to her life at home. Right now, she's glaring at me like I've failed her personally. Like if I couldn't find a way to relax on a Caribbean cruise, maybe I should have let her go in my place.

If only she knew.

Every time my phone buzzes—always a friend texting to see how my trip was—I nearly jump out of my skin. It's never Doug. It's still too soon. But the more I tell myself that, the more I'm less sure I know when it won't be too soon. Another day? A week? A month? Liam and I are so over he doesn't even care that I let myself into his place and took my stuff while he was an ocean away.

How long will it take Doug to unravel his life from Calvin's?

And what if it takes so long the magic from our cruise wears off and he never calls at all? He may realize I'm not husband material after all.

The answers swirl around in my head like white water threatening to pull me under.

I don't know if I'll ever be relaxed again.

This all sucks.

23

DOUG

"I have made a terrible mistake."

I look up from my computer, where I've been staring at the same clown fish screensaver for the last twenty minutes. "What?"

Harpreet is standing in my office door, eyes wide. "I screwed up."

"How?"

She sighs and slumps into one of the chairs across from my desk. Harpreet is in charge of marketing for the film festival. She's a beast and has been on the team almost as long as I have, so I'm sure whatever she's worried about is nothing serious.

Especially when you compare it with how completely I've managed to run my own life aground.

I smooth my hand over the veneer of my desk. The wood is two shades darker than the furniture in our suite on the cruise ship. The office has about as much personality too. We moved into this building while my dad was in the hospital and decorating never felt like a priority. I've got a calendar tacked up on the wall, but it's one of those free calendars they give away to customers at Calvin's bank. The only other thing I've added was a framed photo of Calvin and me at last year's rainbow carpet

185

gala. The second I saw it when I got back from Florida, I stuffed it into a desk drawer, and I haven't managed to look at it since.

Harpreet's still waiting to tell me her tale of woe.

"What happened?" I ask.

She leans forwards like she's about to share a very important secret. "I booked the Malaysian entry to start at three in the morning instead of three in the afternoon."

"And?" We won't start selling tickets until after Christmas, so it's not like we have to reissue anything at this point.

"And they noticed and sent me a very pointed email about disrespecting their art and how difficult it was to get this film made at all."

They're not wrong. Being queer in Malaysia is tough. We're thrilled to have them on the program. But still . . . "Do you want me to write an apology?" I've spent the last three days drowning in my inbox. What's another message?

Harpreet sighs again, hugging one knee towards herself. "No. It's fine. I just wanted to get it off my chest. Their pointed email was, well, super pointy. Patrick's already on top of changing the time. I can send you a draft of my reply to them if you want to see it."

I wave the offer away. She knows exactly how to smooth this over. We have these little hiccups every year. Most of them get fixed before anyone but me and Harpreet notice, but diplomacy is definitely part of the job description.

She smiles as she stands up again. "Your tan's fading."

The idea makes me sick, like I'm losing everything that was good about my honeymoon with it. But I say, "I don't really tan. I just burn."

She gives me a grin. "Well, you were never going to be as brown as me anyway. What are you doing tonight? Finley and I made a bunch of pakoras and put half in the freezer. We can cook them up and watch Ryan Reynolds's greatest hits."

I give her a weak smile. "Not tonight. Thanks, though."

Her expression is concerned, and I wonder how long everyone at the office is going to keep mothering me. But then she says, "He's at the front," and I realize her concern isn't about my tan. It's about my fiancé, who is waiting to take me for lunch.

Ex-fiancé.

"Want me to tell him to go jump out a window?" Harpreet asks.

Desperately. "That's okay." I'll tell him myself.

She gives me a thumbs-up. "The pakora-and-Ryan offer stands."

My whole team has been great since I got home. Harpreet and Nash, our festival director, were at the wedding. They know what happened and have clearly passed on at least the essential details to everyone else at work. It could be embarrassing, but not having to explain it has made the last few days easier.

If only I could explain to them why I let the man who didn't want to marry me close to two weeks ago take me out for lunch every day since I've been back.

That would require me knowing why I'm doing it.

Calvin looks nervous as I approach the office's main doors, and I wish I could take some satisfaction in seeing him like this, but his arrival just makes me tired.

I guess fatigue is better than the sheer horror I felt at the cruise terminal.

Okay, maybe seeing him all penitent and waiting for me is satisfying.

"Doug! Hi." He leaps to his feet as I approach. "How was your morning?"

"It was fine."

He leans in to kiss me, and I turn my head away. Harpreet, Nash, and two other people from our team walk by, and Harpreet gives me a look. It's the *do I need to hurt someone?* look. I smile and wave her off.

Calvin and I walk down to a sandwich place on the corner.

His office isn't that far from mine, but we've never met for lunch before. Now we've eaten together at the same table in the corner for the last three days.

Maybe his sudden attention is because I've refused to move back into the condo, and so these forty-five minutes over my BLT is the only time I've allowed him to have. Being in close proximity to him just leaves me hurt and confused, so I've worked hard to set clear boundaries while I figure out my own feelings.

Tripp would be proud of me.

I shuffle forwards in line at the diner counter, but I'm so lost in memories of Tripp's face, his kind voice as he told me to send up a flare when I was ready to come back to him, that I don't even hear the woman at the cash register ask for my order.

Calvin's voice cuts into my ruminations.

"And he'll have the BLT on white. Not too much mayo." He puts a hand on the small of my back, and I jump before giving the woman a nervous smile.

"Actually," I say with trembling words, "I'll have a—uh—" I scan the chalkboard menu, desperately trying to find something else. "I'll have the hot chicken sandwich."

The woman nods and goes to punch it into the order, but Calvin says, "Sweetie, are you sure?"

I narrow my eyes. "Yes, *dear*. I am." He doesn't get to insert himself where I don't need or want him anymore.

Calvin blinks and takes a step back, and I use the chance to escape from the counter and go sit down. He stays around to pay and then trails after me, carrying two cans of mineral water with him. Every step he takes towards me further ratchets up my anxiety.

"How was work this morning?" he asks. I flinch at the question and how normal it sounds when everything between us is abnormal. He notices, and his eyes narrow. "What?"

"It was fine. Harpreet alienated the Malaysians, but I think she's going to get it back on track."

He reaches for my hand. "Doug. We need to talk."

"I'm not sure I'm ready to talk."

He sighs. "Babe. You haven't been ready to talk since you got off the boat."

"Well whose fault is that? If you hadn't abandoned me on our wedding and thought a text message was enough of an explanation, I'd feel more conversational."

I haven't said that many words in a row to him since Florida. I gave up on finding the limo, because Calvin didn't deserve one. Instead, in the cab that Calvin hailed, I stared out the window, watching Miami flow by. At the airport, I very pointedly bought a pair of big headphones from one of those vending machines that sells everything from earbuds to iPads and wore them until the customs agent in Toronto asked me to take them off so he could make sense of our very confusing tale about how I had been out of the country for more than a week, and Calvin had only flown down to Florida yesterday.

And when Calvin led me to a cab and said, "You'll feel better when we get home," I panicked and said I'd rather go to my mom's and that I'd call him in the morning.

What I should have done was call Tripp.

Tripp and I agreed I needed to sort things out with Calvin, but the more time I spend in Toronto, the more I'm sure that was the wrong decision. I don't need closure with Calvin. There's nothing between us but the lease on the condo. No paperwork to do, no assets to split but some furniture. Who cares why Calvin didn't want to marry me? He didn't, and now I don't want to be married to him.

I just want Tripp.

Our sandwiches are set in front of us, and I know right away I made a mistake. When I saw hot chicken, I envisioned the hot turkey sandwiches my mom makes on Boxing Day: white bread, gravy, maybe some stuffing and mayonnaise.

What I am given makes my eyes water before I even lean in to inspect it. The fumes burn my sinuses. "What is . . ."

Calvin sighs. "Babe, I told you to order the BLT. No way can you handle a Nashville hot chicken."

Nashville? What does that have anything to do with it? I run a finger around the edge of the bun, which is stained red, and stick it in my mouth.

For a second, I think I'll be okay.

And then the pain begins.

"Oh my God." I don't know what to do. It's spreading from my lips over my tongue like a burning fuse. I nearly knock over the can of sparkling water, but manage to catch it with shaking hands and suck it all down in one go, even though all that fizz so quickly makes my stomach hurt. I breathe, taking stock. The heat is still there. It's like I've washed it from a single line until it coats the entire inside of my mouth. "What is that?" I glare at the sandwich.

"I told you that you shouldn't order that." Calvin sighs and opens his drink. "You can't handle spicy things."

If you ask Calvin, there are lots of things I can't handle. Spicy food. Ordering a meal. Planning a wedding. Hell, he gave the cab driver at the airport my mother's address, like I wouldn't be able to navigate my way to the house I grew up in.

Annoyed, I bite into the sandwich and the heat makes me choke. Calvin shifts uncomfortably, like he can't believe he has to sit through this childish display of willfulness. I take another bite and make myself chew carefully before swallowing.

I *can* handle things. Even the hard stuff.

Except it's been three days, and all I've done is avoid Calvin, because I don't know what to say. I go straight from my mom's house to work and back again, where Mom and my sisters guard the front door like gargoyles. Since we got back to

Toronto, Calvin and I have seen each other for a total of an hour and a half plus however many minutes today, and it's all been small talk. I thought I was protecting myself, but every minute I spend sitting at this damn table is a minute I'm not with Tripp.

I take another bite of the sandwich. The spice is so hot I have to cough before I can swallow. Calvin is watching me with raised eyebrows, but I eat more, letting the heat roll over me. It's only pain, just like this conversation with Calvin will be painful. But it will be temporary, and then I'll never have to do it again.

"What the hell happened?" I ask.

He looks surprised at the firm tone of my voice, and that surprise hardens my resolution. It's time. By setting boundaries, I've been protecting myself from more hurt, but those boundaries are keeping me away from the things—the person—I want the most.

"I'm sorry," he says, shoulders drooping.

"You keep saying that, but you haven't actually told me what happened." I pull my phone out. He's sent new texts. In fact, he sent a bunch while I was at sea, but I didn't have the service to receive them. They're a week-long apology, and I am sympathetic, but they don't provide any information I didn't already have.

I scroll through them, back to the one that turned my world on its ear.

Never mind.

I hold the phone out to him, so he can see what he did. "What does this mean?"

His gaze drops to the table, and Calvin picks at the crust of his sandwich. I bite into mine, ignoring the burn that spreads over my lips. When he doesn't say anything, I stand, shaking my head. "That's fine. I'll get the rest of this to go." And buy stock in antacids on my way back to the office.

"I couldn't find my cufflinks," Calvin says.

The answer is so absurd I drop back into my seat. "Excuse me?"

His gaze is guilty and miserable. "On Saturday morning, I went to the barber, had a hot shave, came back to the hotel, got dressed, and realized I must have left my cufflinks somewhere. I looked all over the room. They weren't there."

I stare, disbelieving. My hands shake as I lift the phone again. "And this was your solution?" The last week has been a tidal wave of emotions, but suddenly my sadness seems so pointless. He bailed over a pair of cufflinks. "You have got to be kidding me. I would have married you even without them."

I would have. Ten days, eleven days—however many it's been—ago, I'd have held his hands, floppy cuffs and all, and told everyone we cared about that I was happy to be his husband. Now, I can't even begin to understand why I thought that was a good idea.

"No." He shakes his head sadly. "It wasn't about the cufflinks. Or not completely. It was just the last straw. I'd worked so hard to make everything perfect. It was exhausting."

"It didn't have to be." I bite savagely into what's left of my sandwich, the heat fueling my frustration. "I never asked you for perfect."

"I know. But I wanted to give it to you. Sweetheart. You needed so much care, after your dad died. I knew how much this wedding meant to you and when I couldn't—"

"Meant to *me*? I didn't want the custom invitations and the bespoke suit. That was all you." My voice is rising. People are staring. I didn't mean to have this out in a diner, but here we are.

"But you needed—"

"What do you think I need? You're not my father. I don't need a caretaker. I need a partner."

His smile turns soft, and his words are a mental pat on the head. "I know, honey. You've been doing so much better lately."

Is he even hearing me? Maybe that's the problem. When was

the last time we had a conversation? A real conversation, about ourselves, our hopes. Since he proposed, all our conversations have been about guest lists and seating arrangements. Before we were engaged, we didn't talk. He made sure I didn't die from grief, and I did whatever he said.

"Do you love me?" I ask.

"Doug, honey." Now he really does reach across the table to pat my hand. I leave a red smear of hot sauce on his palm. I hope he rubs it in his eye later. "Of course I do."

"Do you?" We spent so much money on that wedding, and we could have saved it all if we'd only had this conversation sooner. "Because from where I'm sitting, you don't want a husband. You want a project."

He purses his lips and smooths down his tie. "Don't look at it that way. I'm just trying to help you get some of the rust off. You scrub up good when someone pushes you a little."

Did he really just say that?

Except of course he did. He's been saying it all along. I thought it was love. I thought it was caring. And maybe it was, when I was dealing with everything around my dad, but somehow, even when I didn't need that anymore, it had just become our relationship. Calvin was never really my boyfriend. He was someone who wanted to help me be a better, more sophisticated version of myself. A life coach, when I thought he was a partner.

But I know now that someone loves this version of me. The cheese pizza guy. He said I could be more than that, but either way he still loves my jokes, my body. He doesn't laugh when I tell him I'm afraid of heights.

Maybe I needed Calvin when my dad was sick. He was a rock, and I will always be grateful for that, but ours isn't a partnership. It's not equal.

Tripp and I are equals. We push each other, accept each other, and hold hands for the ride instead of pulling the other one along and saying it's for their own good.

I brush my thumb over the gold band on my finger. I was so proud to wear it and call myself someone's husband.

Not Calvin's husband, though. I'd have been his tagalong. His project. Never his husband.

But I was Tripp's. For seven days, I was Doug Chet-Bryson Gillingham-Freeman, and it was everything I wanted to be. And then I let him go.

I push up from my chair. The sandwich is gone, and I'm still here. The pain will fade soon.

"Doug. Please. Let's just talk—" Calvin reaches for me again.

I say, "I have to go. I've made a terrible mistake."

24

TRIPP

The side effect of all this waiting is three positive things happen in that first week back in Vancouver:

Pierce's house has never been so clean. I'm moody as hell and feel guilty for descending on him, so I start to stress clean and basically don't stop.

My website is finally up-to-date. I've got loads of cute photos and videos I've been meaning to share, and now is the perfect time to get them online.

And Trixie has never been so spoiled. We go for walks all over the city and spend hours at dog parks. I buy her an adorable new jacket with a faux fur hood and a squeaky stuffy dolphin that she immediately adores and carries with her everywhere.

It's so good to be home.

"You're overcompensating," Pierce says on Friday morning.

"I am not," I say, more loudly than I should. "What would I be compensating for?" I poke at my melon. It's not as sweet and fresh as what they served on the ship, but I'm trying to stay in the habit of eating breakfast, just in case it really is the most important meal of the day.

And also because breakfast makes me think of Doug, and I don't have much else that does.

Do you know we didn't take one picture together on that whole cruise? Not a single selfie. I have no photos of Doug dozing in a hammock or looking over his shoulder at me with his soft smile. There was that one photo taken of us in Mexico, but I never got around to buying it. All I have are a cascade of hickeys on my neck and chest that made Pierce cackle the first time he saw them as I came out of the shower, and those are fading.

On the third day, I cracked and looked him up online—Doug, not Pierce. Doug's got a Facebook account, but the updates died out a couple years ago, aside from the obligatory birthday wishes. I closed the tab before I could do anything stupid. Sending him a friend request feels like pressuring him, when I promised to wait.

"You're also brooding, along with compensating," Pierce says.

"Would you quit it?"

"Stop glooming around my house like the ghost of a spurned Victorian heiress."

"I'm not—" I growl and push back from my chair. "Forget it. Trix! Come here, Trix. Time for a walk." She hops up from where she's been dozing under our feet and turns in excited circles, her nails clicking on the tile floor. "Yes. Time for a walk! And then we're going to work. You get to see all your friends. Yes, you do, you good girl," I babble as I find the leash in the front hall.

Surprisingly, Pierce follows us, which isn't really his style. Whenever I've turned up at his house before in a heap of broken hearts and dashed hopes, he's usually much more of the tough-love, *what did you think was going to happen?* kind of best friend.

"What do you want to do for dinner tonight?" I ask breezily. "Maybe we can order that basil pork you like?"

"Tripp. You can just call him. It's the twenty-first century."

I shake my head. "I can't. He needs space right now."

"Says who?"

"Says you," I say, desperation pawing at my skin like an impatient dog.

"Me?" Pierce puts a surprised palm to his chest.

"Yes, you." I poke at him. "You're the one always telling me to get the stars out of my eyes and see reality when I meet someone new."

He puffs up in irritation. "I mean that when you bring home the fuckboy whose only talent is giving good head or the alpha male who just wants you for arm candy."

I squawk. "There was more to some of them than that."

At my feet, Trixie growls impatiently and noses at the door.

Pierce rolls his eyes. "Okay, some of them were alpha males *and* gave good head. Don't argue with me." He holds up a finger when I go to do just that. "Your track record is the only evidence I need."

"Exactly. 'Slow down. You don't really know this guy.' That's what you always say."

"And when have I ever been wrong?"

Normally, this is the part where I sulk and say he doesn't understand. That Luca is a diamond in the rough or who is he to judge if Amir *likes* it rough? But then—whether it's a week, or a month—he never holds it over my head when I show up heartbroken at his door and tell him it didn't work out.

"So what's your point?" I ask while Trixie yelps.

He folds his arms over his chest. "At no time have you told me why it's going to work with this guy. In fact, you've hardly said anything about him at all."

"You told me to grow up. Stop dreaming and face reality. Well, I'm doing it, Pierce. I'm trying to give him the space he asked for!" It's the refrain that has been chanting in my head over and over. I asked Doug what he needed, and he chose Calvin. Maybe not forever, but for right now. I have to trust that the promises we made to each other will be enough to bring him back to me when he's ready. I have to trust I am enough.

Trixie grabs hold of one of my shoes at the door and shakes it vigorously. I grind my teeth. "I have to go. My dog is going to pee on your floor if I don't let her outside."

But Pierce isn't letting up. "Every other guy you've ever told me about, you've practically tattooed his name on your ass by the time I meet him, and this time . . . You're so protective. Of him and of yourself . . . "

"What do you want me to do?" My voice is rising, and my throat aches. "This is real life, not some fantasy. Do you think he's going to show up at my door and ask me to give up my lease on the daycare and move to Ontario? That's not how it works!" I shout the last words. I've been doing everything I can to stay calm all week, but with every word my resolve is cracking. Maybe Pierce is right. Maybe I should hop on a plane and fly to Toronto. I'll find the film festival where Doug works and camp outside until he agrees to see me.

Trixie whines at my feet, and a small puddle forms on the boot mat beneath her.

I sigh. "Sorry. Let me put her outside, and I'll clean it up."

"No," Pierce says, deflating under his Patagonia vest. "Sorry. My fault. I shouldn't have pushed."

I pick up my trembling dog, careful of the puddle, and unlock the front door. "It's fine. You're not wrong. I'm just—"

My words are cut off as I swing the door open and Doug is there, eyes wide and embarrassed, like I've just chopped down the shrub he was hiding behind so he could eavesdrop.

"Oh. Hi." His ears are pink, and he's got his coat collar turned up against the drizzle this morning. "I, uh—would you consider giving up your lease at the doggie daycare and moving to Ontario?"

I stare. My chest—all of it, my lungs, my heart, my ribs—is going to burst. His appearance here is impossible, and he looks like a completely different person, dressed up for drizzly BC mornings instead of the Caribbean heat.

But he's here.

Trixie wiggles in my arms.

My feet are rooted to the floor.

"Probably should have eased into that," Doug says.

Now I understand why Trixie wets herself when she gets overly excited. I am barely in control of my bodily functions. I am one big tremble from my toes to my eyelashes, while my brain has gone completely still. All it does is pulse one word on my consciousness like a neon sign.

Doug.

I shove Trixie at him. "I have to walk the dog."

"Oh. Um. Sure." He fumbles, and she growls, but he manages to wrestle her wiggly body against his chest, and she settles, licking his chin once to tell him she's forgiven him.

If only I could do the same.

Something flies by my head, and I realize it's the mat Trixie peed on. It lands on the lawn with a muffled thump. Easier than cleaning it up, I guess.

"Okay!" Pierce says behind me. I'd pretty much forgotten he existed at all. "I have to get to work. Tripp, you've got your key?"

I nod and drag my leaden feet over the threshold. Doug has to back down the steps to make room for us, but he keeps Trixie clutched to him, and for a second I have the ridiculous thought that he's here to dognap her, take her to Toronto, and force me to follow them to get her back.

He must know he doesn't need that much leverage.

A sharp giggle escapes from my mouth. Trixie yips and squirms. Pierce locks the door and gives us a wave as he heads down the street towards the SkyTrain shuttle stop. "Doug, will you be here for dinner? We're having Thai."

"I—" He glances at me. "Maybe?"

"He likes chicken." I can't help myself. I don't even know

what he's doing here, but I need to make sure he's comfortable. "Not too spicy."

"Oh, um." He buries his face in Trixie's ruff, and I hate my dog so much right now. If Doug's going to be buried in anyone, it should be me. "Whatever you guys usually order. I'm sure it'll be fine. Or we could do sushi?"

"Sushi?" I didn't think our last attempt was all that successful.

"Yeah. I like tuna rolls. You have those here, right?"

Pierce laughs. "You text me when you two have come to a decision."

He's not talking about takeout.

We stare at each other until Pierce is out of earshot. Trixie's back legs are paddling frantically. She's a great dog, but she's not much of a cuddler.

"You, uh, you want to put her down? I've got the leash here."

We walk a few blocks in silence. Trixie knows something's up and insists on stopping to sniff every single tree, post, hydrant, and parked car between here and the dog park. It's like she's welcoming Doug to the neighborhood and wants him to know exactly which spots are hers.

"What are you doing here? How did you find me?" I ask as we walk through the gate at the park. I slip off the leash, and Trixie immediately barrels after a squirrel that is halfway up a tree before she even gets to it.

"I, uh. Yeah. Good. And you?" Doug shoves his hands in his pockets, then seems to realize he's said the wrong thing. "Oh, sorry. I, uh . . . looked Pierce up online. Turns out there's only one Chilton-Barnes-Smith in Vancouver, so it actually wasn't that hard. I thought he'd be able to tell me where you were."

"Just 'cause?" My insides are doing a riotous *he's here! he's here!* tap dance, but I'm also on high alert, like Calvin might appear from behind a tree at any moment.

"I broke up with Calvin."

I make a soft whining noise that maybe only Trixie can hear. "Broke up?"

"For real. Not in a text message. To his face, so there would be no misunderstanding."

"Why?" Do I really want to know this? Does it matter? He's here, and he's single.

"Because he didn't want a husband. He wanted a plaything. A doll he could carry around and mold into exactly what he wanted."

"Oh." What am I supposed to say to that?

"Tripp." His face is serious, and even though the city around us is waking up, everything feels perfectly still.

"Yeah?"

"You were a great husband."

I swallow hard to hold back the tears. "So were you."

He glances at my hand, where the titanium band is still sitting, snug on my fourth finger. I cover it self-consciously. I've thought about taking it off so many times in the last few days, but I couldn't make myself do it. The ring is mine, because it holds all my memories of one blissful surreal week with the only man I've ever really wanted to marry.

He twines our fingers together. The gold band is still on his hand, and the two rings slide together. He stares at them for a long time, and I hold my breath.

Then he pulls our hands towards him and gently kisses the knuckles.

"I'm sending up my flare," he says, and I gasp. "I shouldn't have let you go at the airport."

"Yes, you—"

His grip tightens on mine. "No. I shouldn't have. I was surprised, and there was so much going on, but I knew the second we got in the cab that I'd made the wrong choice. Tripp." He pulls me closer. "Meeting you was the best thing to ever happen to me. I don't know what our life is going to look like, but I know it's going to be *ours*. Please. You know that, right?"

How many times have I come to Pierce's with that fever-bright look in my eyes, only to have my heart broken a month later?

"It won't be like the ship," I say.

He stiffens. "Is that what you want?"

Do I? Who wouldn't want endless days of sun, sleep, sex, and Doug curled around me? But it was also so tidy. So contained. Shuttle buses and carefully catered meals and cruise ports that all looked the same even though the countries were different.

"No," I say, but I clasp my free hand over his when he goes to pull away. "It can't be like that. It's too perfect. Too easy." My smile is going to split my face in half. "I want so much more. I want to fight with you and make up with you. I leave dirty dishes on the counter, and I get cranky when I'm cold."

He's smiling too. "I only know how to cook hamburgers, and my underwear drawer is organized by style and colour."

Trixie runs up, like she knows something important is happening. She barks excitedly around our ankles, and I laugh. "I run a doggie daycare, and my own dog is only like sixty percent housetrained."

Doug's nose wrinkles. "I'm afraid of cats."

Good enough for me. I lean in, unable to stop myself, and our kiss is perfect in the grey Vancouver morning. His beard is soft, his lips firm, and he groans. He made the same sound on the ship, and I will never get tired of it, no matter where we are.

"How long are you here for?" I ask breathlessly.

"Sunday morning. I can't take more time off work."

We'll have to stay up all weekend to make up for lost time.

I take him downtown. The daycare is supposed to be opening in five minutes, so we rush up the street. Several dogs and their owners have already gathered at the door. Cherise is there too, but I'm the one with the key.

"I'm here, I'm here!" I've got Trixie's leash around one wrist and Doug's hand held tight.

"We were starting to worry," someone says. I push through the group, fumbling for my keys without letting go of Doug. Soft doggy noses sniff at our knees and calves, but I push forwards like nothing is amiss. Most of my clients are long-term, and they know I have never brought anyone to work with me.

Monica—whose Boston terrier, Didi, is a terror—says, "Who's this? New employee?"

I glance at Doug, and he gives me his bravest smile.

"Tell them whatever you want," he says.

So I turn to the people I see every day, and who are some of the best people I know, because they're great to their dogs, and proudly, I say, "This is my husband, Doug. We just got back from our honeymoon."

DOUG

Four months later…

"You ready?" Tripp pokes his head into the bedroom.

I smooth the lapels on my suit jacket down. The pants don't fit as well as they did before Christmas. Somehow, I thought all those mornings walking Trixie would pay off, but it turns out they don't counterbalance the way Tripp is determined to eat at every restaurant in the city. Fortunately, almost all of them have chicken.

Still, the jacket fits fine, but I'm feeling nervous. I turn to Tripp, holding out my tie. "Can you help me?"

He gives me a sympathetic expression, but he gets the knot done with just a few flicks of his wrist. Tripp's gone for something more casual. Collared shirt with the top two buttons open. Midnight-blue velvet tuxedo jacket. It's the perfect colour for his eyes.

"There." He kisses my nose. "All set."

When he goes to take a step back, I reach for him to kiss him again. He laughs against my lips. "Doug. We have to go."

We do. The opening rainbow carpet for the festival starts in an hour. On a Friday night in the city, the drive alone could take a half hour, and I can't be late. But Tripp's mouth against mine and his sunshine and coconut scent—turns out it wasn't just the piña coladas; he's got coconut shampoo too—are hard to tear myself away from.

His hand's on my zipper, and I purr, pleased he's getting with the program.

"Your fly's down," he says, tugging at my earlobe with his teeth.

I roll my eyes and stumble back, fumbling to get my pants done up properly.

Trixie's waiting for us at the door, and she trots an impatient circle as we put on our coats. Winter is almost over, but it's not warm enough to go out in just our formalwear. Tripp glares at me as he does his parka up to his chin. The transition from Vancouver's grey drizzle to Toronto's damp freeze has not been an easy one, and he reminds me regularly that he's only putting up with it because he loves me.

But he loves me a lot and spring is just around the corner, so I think we'll be okay.

"No, pretty girl." Tripp bends down to rub Trixie's toasted marshmallow head. "You're not coming." She growls and shakes her head, and he laughs.

We grab an Uber, and the car makes its way downtown. Tripp bounces a knee as he stares out the window at Toronto's glowing skyline.

"You'll be fine," I say, putting a hand on his thigh.

"I've never done a red carpet before."

"I'm just the programming director." We got dressed up because why not? But no one is going to stop us for a photo or ask who we're wearing. It's not the Oscars or even the Toronto International Film Festival. We'll be under the radar from beginning to end. No reason to be nervous.

"Remind me of their names again?"

Tripp's met some of my co-workers since he arrived in Toronto a few months ago, but he's been so busy getting settled and finding clients for the new daycare that I can't say I blame him for not remembering.

"There's Nash, the festival director, and his boyfriend, Brady. And Harpreet, who runs marketing, and her partner, Finley."

He nods but doesn't look all that confident. Tripp tangles his fingers in mine, and I press my lips to his knuckles.

His arrival hasn't been perfect. He really does leave dirty dishes on every imaginable surface. And he's a misery in the morning before he's had coffee. Being rumpled and semi-communicative was one thing on a cruise ship where we could eat breakfast at our leisure while the sun rose. Trying to get him out of bed and off to work, particularly when it's thirty below out, has been a trial.

But he kisses me goodbye before he leaves for the day and then again when we get home from work. He holds my hand as we walk Trixie, and he cheers loudest when I take him to trivia night at the brew pub near our new condo, even if he only knows half the answers.

He doesn't need all the answers. Not when he has me.

The rainbow carpet is more like a reception than a parade. We're on one of the upper floors of the TIFF building down-town. In the end, we're early, so the space is still mostly empty. Patrick, who works for Harpreet in marketing, is seated at a long table, surrounded by stacks of name tags.

"Hi, Doug," he says with a smile.

"Patrick."

"One second." He goes through the name tags but frowns as he gets down the stack. "I don't see you here."

"Try in the Gs," I say.

He glances at me, eyes wide behind his thick glasses, then his smile broadens. "Right." His fingers flip through the pile until he says, "Oh, here it is." He hands me a name tag. "And that means you must be Tripp." He passes Tripp his name tag too.

Tripp is still looking nervous, but his posture relaxes when he sees the name on my tag.

Doug Gillingham-Freeman, Programming Director

"I thought we agreed on Freeman-Gillingham," he says, eyes narrowed playfully, but he slips his own lanyard over his head.

I shrug. "Clerical error."

We did decide on Freeman-Gillingham, but I feel like there can be some flexibility in unofficial documents. And anyway, we've only been married for four days, so I can be excused for mixing them up while I get used to it. It's a mouthful, in whichever order you say it.

"Doug!" Nash is striding towards us. The festival director is my friend, but he's still imposing in his black tuxedo.

"Hi Nash. Brady." I nod at Nash's boyfriend, who stands half a step behind him. The two of them are funny, and I still haven't figured out their dynamic, but Brady seems to know when Nash needs his moment to shine.

"Tripp." Nash shakes Tripp's hand. "Nice to see you again."

"You too." Tripp stands a bit straighter in his velvet jacket.

"And I guess congratulations are in order."

Tripp gives me a shy smile. "I guess. Doesn't really feel like anything's changed."

We got married on a Tuesday. I left the office an hour early, despite all the pre-festival chaos, and Tripp got someone to watch the dogs. We went to City Hall and did it. My mom and sisters and Pierce were there, along with Tripp's parents and stepmother. They seem nice but distant, like they don't know what to make of their son who moved across the country for someone he'd only spent a week with and is marrying only a few months later.

But, when you know, you know. All common wisdom said we should take our time. Let Tripp get settled, make sure we have enough in common to fill more than a luxury suite and a beach bag of sex toys.

Tripp said we should wait, but when I asked why, he said, "I want you to be sure."

I was sure. I am a cheese pizza kind of guy. Risk is not my wheelhouse. But with Tripp, I don't see risk. I see adventure. I see white water that will take me where I want to go, as long as I keep my toes pointed in the right direction.

Tripp is that direction. Dirty dishes and all.

I put a hand on his back, wishing it was just skin instead of smooth velvet. I say, "Brady, meet my husband, Tripp."

Brady says, "Great to meet you. Congratulations on the wedding. Are you taking your honeymoon once the festival is over?"

Tripp leans into my touch, like his nerves have finally floated away on a salt-scented breeze.

"We've already been on our honeymoon," I say.

Brady frowns. "Already? Must have been fast. That doesn't seem fair."

Tripp takes my hand in both of his, the white-gold band on his finger brushing over the yellow one on mine. We talked about keeping the titanium ring, but it was the one Calvin picked out, and in the end, we wanted our rings to be only ours.

"Trust me," he says to Brady. "The trip was perfect."

Everyone should fall in love on their honeymoon.

THANK YOU

Thank you so much for reading *Honeymoon Sweet*. If you missed it, don't forget to check out Nash and Brady's steamy and sweet office romance in Work-Love Balance.

Follow me on Amazon to be notified of new releases, or come join my Facebook readers group (facebook.com/groups/allisonsalist). Or sign up for The A-List (allisontemplebooks.com/newsletter), my monthly newsletter for new releases, giveaways, and recommendations.

The kindest thing a reader does for an author is read their book. The second kindest is to recommend it. Please take a minute to leave a review on Amazon or Goodreads, so other readers will know if this story is for them!

ABOUT THE AUTHOR

Whether I knew it then or not, I've been a writer since the second grade, when I wrote a short story about a girl and her horse. My grandmother typed it out for me and said she'd never seen so many quotation marks from a seven-year-old before. I took that as a challenge and have tried to break that record in all the stories I've taken on since then. It's good to have goals, right?

I live in Toronto with my very patient husband and the world's neediest cat. I try to split my time between writing, community theatre stage management, and traveling anywhere that has good wine. Tragically, this leaves no time to clean the house.

ALSO BY ALLISON TEMPLE

Out & About
Work-Love Balance

The Seacroft Stories
Top Shelf
Cold Pressed
Hot Potato

Standalone
The Pick Up

www.ingramcontent.com/pod-product-compliance
Lightning Source LLC
Chambersburg PA
CBHW071401100726
47908CB00004B/1060